The Black Diamond Cartel

Lock Down Publications and Ca$h
Presents
The Black Diamond Cartel
A Novel by *SAYNOMORE*

The Black Diamond Cartel

Lock Down Publications
P.O. Box 944
Stockbridge, Ga 30281

Visit our website @
www.lockdownpublications.com

Copyright 2023 by SAYNOMORE
The Black Diamond Cartel

This is a work of fiction. Names, characters, places, and incidents either are products of the author's imagination or are used fictitiously. Any similarity to actual events or locales or persons, living or dead, is entirely coincidental.

Lock Down Publications
Like our page on Facebook: Lock Down Publications @
www.facebook.com/lockdownpublications.ldp

Book interior design by: **Shawn Walker**
Edited by: **Kiera Northington**

Stay Connected with Us!

Text **LOCKDOWN** to 22828 to stay up-to-date with new releases, sneak peaks, contests and more...

Thank you!

Submission Guideline

Submit the first three chapters of your completed manuscript to ldpsubmissions@gmail.com, subject line: Your book's title. The manuscript must be in a .doc file and sent as an attachment. Document should be in Times New Roman, double spaced and in size 12 font. Also, provide your synopsis and full contact information. If sending multiple submissions, they must each be in a separate email.

Have a story but no way to send it electronically? You can still submit to LDP/Ca$h Presents. Send in the first three chapters, written or typed, of your completed manuscript to:

LDP: Submissions Dept
Po Box 944
Stockbridge, Ga 30281

DO NOT send original manuscript. Must be a duplicate.

Provide your synopsis and a cover letter containing your full contact information.

Thanks for considering LDP and Ca$h Presents.

ACKNOWLEDGMENTS

First, I would like to thank God and my Lord and Savior Jesus Christ for all the blessings on my life, and for walking me through all of my hard times. Much respect and love goes out to the Lock Down Publications family. Big shoutout goes to Ca$h, hands down. Love, bruh.

I want to acknowledge everyone who had a hand in this project, from the cover designer and layout person to the editor and proofreader. Thanks to all of you.

Much love goes to my godson Rashad aka Shade. I love you, baby boy. I look at you like you are my own son. From the time you came into this world, you was a star in my eyes. Facts!

Lock Down Publications, in my DJ Khaled voice, WE DA BEST.

The soldier who knows not when to strike or to yield, will never taste the sweetness of victory but know only the bitterness of defeat.

~Unknown~

The Black Diamond Cartel

SAYNOMORE

Prologue

"Do you mind if I smoke in here, Mr. Lake?" Mr. Lake got up from the side of the table and walked to the window and opened it. After taking a deep breath, he looked at Malachi.

"No. I don't mind, but do you mind stepping to the window, so the smell won't get all over my office?" Malachi got up and walked to the two sided window, and looked at the city of New York as he pulled out a cigar and lit it.

"Now tell me everything this so-called bull District Attorney Cox has against me, Mr. Lake." Mr. Lake sat at the table and opened up Malachi's file.

"For starters, they have a strong witness against you, that said you have ordered a multitude of hits, and to prove his point, he has shown the D.A. and police burial locations, where they already un-buried three bodies. First victim's name, Alex Moore, a thirty-four-year-old white male, cause of death was a gunshot to the back of the head. Then we have Walter Stone, a black male, cause of death was his neck was cut from ear to ear. And the last victim, Crystal Smith, cause of death shot three times in the chest." Attorney Lake took his reading glasses off and placed them on the table as he looked at Malachi.

"So, three dead bodies come up, and somebody's saying I ordered the hits. It's my word versus theirs. If they know where the bodies were at, then they are the ones who are guilty of the murders, not me." Malachi continued to pull on his cigar as he looked out the window.

"You know District Attorney Cox has multitude pictures of victims. You are being charged with three counts of murder, three counts of kidnapping, three counts of aggravated assault, three counts of extortion, three counts of organized crime. They have you as the ringleader, and it's no secret you have New York in a strong-hold. The only reason you are out on bail is because I called in a hundred favors." Malachi flicked his cigar out the window and walked back to the table and sat across from Mr. Lake.

"So, paint a picture for me here, what am I facing?"

"If we lose trial, you are looking at the death penalty and right now, the D.A.'s case is very strong against you." Malachi took his hand and ran it down his face as he took a deep breath.

"Just do your part for me, Mr. Lake and I will take care of the witness. Remember, no witness, no case."

"I'll do my best."

"That's all I'm asking you for." Malachi got up and shook Mr. Lake's hand before leaving his office and walked out to the waiting room where he had Kareem and Bishop waiting for him. He nodded at both of them as he walked out the attorney's office. Mr. Lake watched them leave from his office door.

Chapter 1

Two years earlier, before the murder trial

"We coulda made a lot of money together, the only thing you had to do is let me be a part of your project. Imagine the doors that coulda been opened for the two of us. I came to your office respectfully and talk to you like a man, and what you do? The ultimate disrespect, you went to the police and told them about our conversation. You told them I was trying to extortion you with threats. Now look at you." Malachi walked up to Terry White and looked into his eyes as he lit his cigar.

"Let me tell you something about myself. I don't make threats, I make promises. When I told you I wanted in on the project, or your picture would be on the back of a milk carton or posted up in the entrance of Walmart on the wall, I meant it. What them posters say? Have you seen me? Jaheem, take the tape off of his mouth, I think Mr. White wants to say something." Malachi smoked his cigar as Jaheem took the tape off his mouth.

"You got something you want to say, Mr. White?"

"I have a wife and three children. I was doing what I thought was best for my children, my family." Terry had tears in his eyes and his voice was shaky. He was scared and his eyes were the size of half-dollar coins as he looked at the gallon of gas on the floor. Malachi saw the fear in his eyes as he looked at the gallon of gas.

"The project I wanted to be a part of is over now, the police know about it. An investigation will come up on my part. It will just be a big headache and I really don't want to deal with it now." Malachi nodded at Jaheem. Jaheem picked up the gallon of gas and walked over to Terry and started to pour the gas all over him. Terry started to yell out of fear.

"No! No, please! No, don't do this! I have a family! No, I'm sorry!"

"Me too." Malachi walked up to Terry and flicked his lighter and threw it on him. He watched as he yelled and burst into a hot blaze of fire, then pulled his gun out and shot him three times in the chest, killing him.

"Come on, let's get out of here, I have a two pm appointment with someone very important that I don't want to be late for."

Chapter 2

Kareem walked with Jazmine to the front of Admiral's Row Apartments.

"Kareem, why are we here at this broke down apartment project? This place been closed for years."

"Malachi owns this place, that's why we are here."

"Wait, he purchased these broke down ass buildings?"

"Yeah, you don't see the vision he has for this place, it's in the heart of the city." Kareem and Jazmine walked into the building.

"Kareem, the only vision I see for this place is a wrecking ball."

"Jazmine, open your eyes. Millions are going to come into these doors, with this apartment, we hold the keys to the streets."

"How long before this place is up and running?"

"The contractor said he can have this place up and running within six months, they start working tomorrow."

"So, who is going to be here?"

"We all are, there is going to be cameras on every floor, four security stations. Now come on, let's get out of here. I just wanted to see how this place looked before they start working tomorrow." Jazmine looked around one more time before walking out with Kareem.

***

Malachi pulled up in the front of the building and stepped out of the car. He looked around as he fixed his tie and suit jacket as he walked into the building to the fifth floor. When he opened the door, he saw all eyes looking at him.

"Malachi come inside and have a seat. We have been waiting for you." Malachi looked around at everyone at the table before taking his seat.

"Gentlemen, thanks for waiting. How are y'all doing this evening."

"We are all fine, Malachi, now let us all get to the point of this meeting. Malachi, your men went and threatened Pete's auto part store on 114th Street."

"Ok and what is your point, Mr. Washington?"

"That is Peter's turf. That's my point, Malachi, and that can start unnecessary problems. And don't nobody want that, Malachi." Malachi pulled a cigar out and ran it under his nose. He inhaled it before lighting it. He pulled his cigar and blew the smoke in the air.

"Peter needs to know 114th is my block and any store that's on my block owes me, that corner is my corner."

"What is one corner to keep peace, Malachi?"

"With the utmost respect to you, Mr. Washington, same thing with you Mr. Grunt and you as well, Mr. Lee, but nobody helped me get where I am today. I did it by myself, with blood in the streets. I killed more motherfuckers in the streets of New York than everyone at this table. I ain't get a pass. Now that I have Brooklyn in the headlock and it's a gold mine, everybody wants to move in and if they want to move into my city it comes with a price, money or blood."

"So, you are bigger than the mob now, Malachi?"

"No, Mr. Lee, but I ain't afraid of them motherfuckers, they bleed just like me and you." Malachi looked at everyone at the table with his hazy eyes after he said that.

"Malachi, you won't win every war that comes your way." Mr. Washington leaned back in the chair and crossed his arms after saying that. Mr. Grunt got up and walked to Malachi.

"Malachi, walk with me to the window, let me show you something." Both of them walked to the window after Malachi put his cigar into the astray.

"Malachi, you know what I see when I look out this window at Brooklyn?"

"No, tell me, what do you see?"

"Hell, now when you look at this room, at us, we sat on top of hell in the clouds. You can even call it heaven if you wish." Malachi looked at the room and both men seated at the table, then at Mr. Grunt.

"You are right, Mr. Grunt, but this is how I see things. In heaven there is only one ruler, and no one in this room is the ruler. But in Brooklyn, or hell as you call it, I'm the alpha and omega, the beginning and end. I'd rather be the ruler in hell than the do-boy in heaven, Tell Peter I said everyone pays dues in Brooklyn, with that being said, y'all have a nice day."

"Malachi, you are forgetting one thing." Malachi stopped and looked at Mr. Washington.

"And what's that?"

"The devil got thrown out of heaven down to earth and when the time comes, even he would be killed in his kingdom he calls hell." Malachi smiled at Mr. Washington as he put his sunglasses on and walked away.

"Washington, what are you going to do with your dog?"

"Lee, I can control Malachi, he read between the lines of what I just told him."

"You gave your dog Brooklyn and let him off the leash, now he feels he can piss on any block he wants. That's the thing about these niggas, you give them an inch and they take a mile." Washington got up from the table and looked at both men.

"Like I said, Malachi knows what line to cross and what bridge to burn. I'll see y'all both later and like I said, I will deal with Malachi." Washington put his coat on and walked out the office doors.

Chapter 3

"Detective Oldham. Where do you know this guy from? I'll wait till you tell me." Detective Oldham walked up to the John Doe and kneeled down and looked at him, he took a napkin and covered his mouth as he looked at the burned body.

"You got to be fucking kidding me. Detective Benlose, this is Terry White, he came by the station a few days ago saying that Malachi Williams came to his place of business and threatened him." Detective Oldham walked back next to Detective Benlose.

"How long has he been missing for?"

"He hasn't been reported missing. Some schoolkids found his body and called it in. From the looks of it, if I was to guess, I would say twenty-four hours at the most."

"So, you think we need to have a talk with Malachi Williams, Detective Benlose?"

"Yeah, but let's wait a little while and see how he moves. Malachi has a lot of friends in high places. So, if we want to get him, we have to do it the old school way, two cops and a badge."

"And we should also look at Terry White's business partner, to make sure he ain't sell him out and make a deal with Malachi behind his back."

"Good point, let's check into that now."

***

The 2022 Genesis G70 2.0T sedan pulled up in front of the brownstone. Jazmine stepped out looking like a runway model, with her long, jet-black hair, honey brown eyes and caramel skin, with her hourglass body. Jazmine was bad and she knew it. She was running neck-in-neck with Beyoncé and Cardi B. She had on skintight faded blue jeans with rips in them, black two-inch red bottom shoes, a Louis Vuitton black belt and a sky-blue Louis Vuitton shirt that hugged her C-cup breasts. Her nails were painted white. Jazmine was a boss bitch and she carried herself like one as she walked into the brownstone. As she looked at all the females with nothing on, breaking up the cocaine on the table, all eyes were on her as she looked at Bishop walking up to her.

"Bishop, you are just the pretty boy, curly black hair, white smile, goatee and brown eyes."

"Come on, stop, beautiful. I got what you are looking for over here." Jazmine walked with Bishop over to the next room, where there was a table with stacks of money on it, Jazmine smiled.

"You like what you see, Jazmine?" Bishop leaned against the door frame and looked at her.

"Yes, I do, this is what you call the American Dream. How much is on the table?"

"Six hundred thousand from last week. I'll have someone place the money into two duffle bags and put it in the trunk of your car." Jazmine turned around and rubbed her hands together.

"That works for me, I'll be outside waiting." Jazmine walked out the brownstone and looked around as Bishop's men walked the duffle bags to her car.

"Jazmine, everything is in the bags. I'll have another pick-up ready for you next week sometime."

"Ok, pretty boy, you know my number when you are ready to see me." Bishop smiled when she said that. He watched as she got into the car and drove off before walking back into the brownstone. Jazmine pulled her phone out and called Kareem. After a few rings, he picked up. Jazmine was looking in her rearview mirror as she talked over the phone.

"Hey, I just made the pick-up from pretty boy, I'm on my way to the car shop now," Jazmine looked into the rearview mirror and saw a black SUV following her two cars back.

"Ok, Malachi is over there right now, I'll call him and let him know you are on your way over there with the pick-up."

"Ok, thanks. Kareem, let me call you back."

Kareem had a feeling something wasn't right. He heard it in Jazmine's voice.

"Jazmine, is everything alright?"

"I don't know, I think there is a black SUV following me. I'm not for sure." Jazmine pulled her Glock 40 out of her purse as she looked into the rearview mirror. She was about to come to a stop at the red light.

"Jazmine, where are you at?"

"I'm at the red light on 127th and…" Jazmine saw the men in the black SUV putting the murder one masks on. Jazmine started talking to herself. "Y'all niggas got me fucked up."

Jazmine opened up her car door and stepped out, gun in her hand and started shooting at the driver of the black SUV, shooting him in the head through the windshield. The passenger side door opened and one of the guys jumped out the truck and started shooting at Jazmine. As she ran and ducked down on the side of her car, you heard people yelling and jumping out of their cars, running so they wouldn't get shot.

Jumping from the side of her car, she looked at the man holding the gun and shot him three times in the chest, dropping him. She watched as his body hit the ground then ran to her car and got into it and drove off. The last man that was in the SUV shot at her car as she drove off, shooting her back window out. Kareem was yelling her name into her earbuds.

"Jazmine! Jazmine, what the fuck is going on?"

"Someone was trying to jack me, I killed two of them. Let me call you back, they shot out my back window."

"Get to the car shop now."

"I'm on my way there now." Jazmine hung up the phone thinking, *how did they know about the pick-up and who tried to set me up?*

SAYNOMORE

Chapter 4

Peter sat in his office behind his desk with two stress balls in his hand, looking out the window as it rained, when Walter walked into his office.

"What do you have to tell me, Walter?"

Walter walked to the bar in Peter's office and poured them two glasses of brandy. He walked over and placed them down as he took his seat in front of the desk.

"I just got done talking to Mr. Grunt." Peter placed the stress balls in his desk drawer and picked up the glass of brandy Walter brought him and took a sip.

"And what did Mr. Grunt have to say?"

"That Malachi is a wild dog off the leash and needs to be put down, because he said 114th is his block and everyone pays dues."

"You know I never liked that nigga. When Washington convinced Lee and Grunt to give Malachi Brooklyn, I knew it would be all bad, but you know what? Mr. Grunt made a good point. It's time to put the stray dog down, and to let Brooklyn know who the fuck I am. I think you need to have a talk with Green." Walter picked up his glass of brandy, drank it with one gulp and placed it back down on the desk.

"I'll go talk with Green now." Walter got up from the chair and walked out of Peter's office. Peter hated to be disrespected and for Walter to say Grunt told him that Malachi wanted him to pay dues was a spit in the face. What made it more disrespectful in his eyes is it came from a nigga.

***

"As I sit at this table I want to know, how the fuck did these muthafuckers know that Jazmine was making a pick-up? and where the fuck was your security that was supposed to be on the block? Bishop, ain't nobody see a big ass black SUV with three niggas in it just posted the fuck up?" Bishop looked at Malachi with nothing to say.

"Jazmine, did you see anyone's face?"

"No Kareem, I just saw them following me and I got on point, shot first, asked questions later." Malachi got up from the table and walked around everyone at the table, until he found himself looking out the window.

"Everyone needs to be tightening up because a storm is headed our way. You have the three crackers that sit above us at the high table looking down on us, then you have Peter Drews, who is trying to move in on one of my blocks." Malachi turned around and looked at everyone at the table.

"Now is not the time for us to be slipping, there is too much on the table at stake right now. As of right now, Bishop, I want twice the security on the block. Cordial, find out who tried to hit us and the third motherfucker who got away. Kill him, find him and kill him. Jaheem… from this point on, every time Jazmine do a pick-up, I want you with her. Kareem, I want you to oversee everything. I have my hands full with the Admiral's Row Apartments project but right now, Cordial, I need that nigga dead."

"Say no more, I'm on it. I'ma rock that baby to sleep on sight."

"There's nothing else to talk about on that note then. I want y'all all at this table to remember this, we are all we got. I'ma lie for you. I'ma ride for you. I'ma die for you. You know why? Because we are family, and family sticks together." Malachi looked around at the table once more before nodding and walking out of the room.

Chapter 5

Bishop had on a black tee-shirt, with some black sweatpants and a black New York baseball cap on, with some black Timberland boots, along with a Glock 40. He had a six-man security team on the block. Kareem told him to move the dope house to a new location. He didn't trust the block anymore, and anything could happen, from the police hitting them, to niggas with a death wish trying to kick in the door. So, the best thing to do was to move the spot to be on the safe side.

"How much more do we have in the spot to load up?"

"Two more truckloads, that's it, then we are done, Bishop."

Bishop looked at Solo and nodded as Solo walked back into the spot to finish getting the boxes to load up the truck. He felt his phone going off, he picked up his phone and saw it was Kareem calling him.

"What's good, homie?"

"Getting the rest of the work out the spot. I should be done in another hour or so."

"Good, keep me posted, I want to know when you are done."

"Copy that." Bishop hung up the phone and finished watching the block. He was mad that someone was laying on his block, trying to lick him and he didn't see it coming. He promised himself the next motherfucker was going to die by his own hands. He looked around one more time before going back into the spot.

***

"Come on, let's go see what this cracker is talking about. If he ain't talking right or got that bread, Malachi said roll his ass, there ain't no more talking, Casper."

"Fuck it, let's do this then." Jaheem and Casper got out of the yellow Hummer and walked into the auto parts store. A few people were walking around the lobby as they walked up to the counter. Jaheem looked at JD.

"Yo-yo, tell me something good, JD." JD looked at Jaheem and Casper.

SAYNOMORE

"You two again? Let me tell you two niggas something. Peter ain't paying no niggas shit to be on this corner, so run back and tell that porch monkey Malachi, Peter said eat a fucking banana. Now you two can get the fuck out of my auto parts shop." Jaheem smiled and looked at JD and shook his head.

"No, cracker, you just fucked up and you are going to deliver a message to that motherfucking cracker Peter without talking." JD looked at Casper as he pulled his gun out and pointed it at him. Jaheem pulled his gun out and shot JD in the chest. As he fell behind the counter, Casper ran up to him and shot him six more times in the chest. People started yelling and running out of the auto parts store. Jaheem looked at JD's dead body, lying behind the counter on the floor in a pool of blood, before walking out of the auto parts store with Casper. Jaheem pulled his phone out and called Malachi, after a few rings he picked up.

"Baby boy got rocked to sleep, and Peter going to get the message." Casper poured gas all over the store then lit a match, setting the store on fire.

"Good, that's what the fuck I wanted to hear, when you fuck with me you end up dead."

"You say get them. I say got 'em."

"Copy that, I'll see you when you touch down, baby boy."

"Already." Jaheem hung up the phone and lit up a blunt as Casper drove off.

***

Walter called Peter from the auto parts shop as he looked down at JD's dead body, and saw the place was on fire.

"JD is dead. I'm looking at his body, they did a number on him, Peter. They set the place on fire, but the guys put it out before it got too bad." Peter had both stress balls in his hand as he talked to Walter over the phone.

"Get everything out of there and call it in, I have a call to make."

"Taking care of that now, boss."

24

"Let me know when you are done." Peter hung up the phone and called Mr. Grunt. Mr. Grunt picked up his phone as he smoked on his cigar and sipped on a glass of brandy.

"Mr. Drews, how may I help you?" Mr. Grunt had his legs crossed as he sat in the chair.

"Malachi crossed the line. He killed my man JD at the auto parts shop on 114th."

"Are you sure it's Malachi?"

"Let's not fool ourselves, Grunt, we know it was him. Now it's my turn to hit back."

"Before you do that, let me call Washington and Lee, we don't need an all-out war right now, Peter."

"Who cares if I kill a nigga, he's not one of us."

"Mr. Grunt, let me break it down this way to you. A tiger will always be a tiger, no matter what. Even if it gets mud on its stripes, the stripes will always be there, meaning it will always be a tiger. And in so many ways what I'm saying is you need to let Williams know Malachi will always be a nigga. Mr. Grunt, with all due respect, we tried it your way. Now, we do it my way. I'm sending my shooters."

"It sounds like to me your mind is already made up."

"It was made up a year ago, but out of respect I let one year pass. Now it's my turn, and I hope y'all of the table respect that."

"I'll be in touch, Peter." Mr. Grant hung up the phone after saying those words and put his hand on his forehead as if he was in deep thought.

***

"What's up, little nigga, you want today to be your payday?" The little homie looked up at Cordial as he sat on the steps, smoking a Newport and rolling a blunt.

"I don't know you, to take your word on a payday. I ain't never seen you before." Cordial nodded and leaned forward.

"That's the best type of money to make, with motherfuckers you don't know, so you will never see them again. The best type of friend to have is a ghost, baby boy. I got ten racks, you trying to eat or what?" Cordial pulled the money out and showed him.

"Shit, what the fuck I have to do?"

"You know where Church Avenue is a few blocks over?"

"Yeah, I know where that block is at, you talking about them brownstones?"

"Yeah, that's a fact, so you know the block I'm talking about."

"Yeah, what about it?"

"A few days ago, niggas tried to hit a spot over there. Shit went zero to a hundred, fast. Two niggas got bodied, one nigga got away. I'm looking for the nigga who got away."

"How I know this shit ain't going to come back against me, real talk?"

"Because I don't need niggas to know who the fuck I talk to, you feel me?" Cordial passed the money to the nigga on the steps. He looked at all the hundreds then put the money in his pocket.

"You looking for Mac Town, that nigga's in Ghosttown on Popping Avenue. Black nigga, full beard, Rick Ross looking ass nigga, he stay with a Pelle Pelle on."

"Little nigga, I hope what you telling me is right, because I'll have to put two niggas in a body bag if you are lying to me. Here, take my number, just in case that nigga come back around here and if he do, call my line." Cordial passed him his number before walking away. Cordial pulled his phone out and called Malachi, after a few rings he picked up.

"I hope you have good news to tell me."

"I do. I found out who this nigga is. I'm on my way to Popping Avenue in the Bronx."

"Keep me posted and take that nigga head off his shoulders."

"Copy that." Cordial hung up the phone and got into his car and drove off.

***

"Detective Oldham, Detective Benlose, come in and tell me what you have so far." Captain Fuller sat behind his desk as Detective Oldham pulled out a notepad and started going over notes.

"We had a talk with Terry White's business partner, he said Terry White had two meetings with Malachi Williams, but that's all he knows."

"Do you think he played a part in his murder?" Detective Oldham looked at Detective Benlose when the captain asked that question.

"No, honestly, I think he had nothing to do with it. What we need to do, sir, is put a team on Malachi now before he becomes too powerful." Captain Fuller tapped his fingers on his desk as Detective Benlose was talking.

"There are bigger fish in the sea right now that we need to focus on."

"With all due respect, like who, sir?" Captain Fuller stopped tapping his fingers on his desk when Detective Benlose asked him that question.

"For starters, you have Peter Drews, who's had a strong hold on New York City, Malachi Williams is a thug running a few blocks. His time is coming but the mayor or chief will not put the money or man power behind an investigation on Malachi Williams. It's just not going to happen."

"Captain, I'm telling you now, Malachi Williams is on the rise as being Mr. Untouchable if we don't stop him now."

"Detective, this conversation is over about Malachi Williams. Both of you focus on your old cases and as far as Terry White goes, until we find out more, it's just another cold case. That will be all, Detectives." Both detectives got up and walked out of Captain Fuller's office and back to their office.

SAYNOMORE

Chapter 6

Malachi walked into the club with Jaheem and Kareem, the DJ gave him a shout out when he saw him. People were walking up to him, dapping him up. Once he made it to the VIP seats, he ordered two bottles of Cîroc on ice, pulled out a cigar and lit it.

"Look around, you see the love we get? We are about to take over New York City. Peter Drews got my fucking message. I ain't playing with nobody, you step on my shoes, I cut your motherfucking throat. I want both of you to remember this. Motherfuckers only respect violence and I will do what the fuck I need to do to get my point across." Malachi reached for the bottle of Cîroc as the waiter walked up to the VIP booth with them.

"Malachi, if motherfuckers only respect violence, Let's show them they can bleed then."

"Let's drink to that, Kareem." Malachi passed the bottle of Cîroc to Kareem.

Both of them said at the same time, "Motherfuckers only respect violence."

"Kareem, let's talk business for a second." Kareem leaned forward to hear what Malachi had to say.

"Kareem, Admiral's Row will be up and running within the next five months. This is a big move for us. I need you to have your A game all the way up. We have no room for mistakes."

"You know my A-game is on, I'm always going to bring it to the court."

"That's why I fuck with you the way I do." Malachi dapped Kareem up and smiled.

"Motherfucker, you are my brother, always."

"I already know, Kareem…likewise, family."

"Yo, I'm about to go to this bathroom. You good?"

"Yeah, I'm good, homie. I have Jaheem standing guard."

"Cool, I'll be right back." Kareem got up and walked to the bathroom as Malachi and Jaheem were in the VIP drinking and bopping their heads to the music.

There were two guys with long coats on, sitting at the bar a few feet from the VIP, looking at Malachi with the bottle of Cîroc in his hand as he took shots from the bottle. They both nodded at each other and got up. By the time Malachi saw them their guns were out, and bullets were flying his way. Malachi flipped over the table backwards from the impact of the bullets. Jaheem pulled his gun out and started shooting back, hitting one of the guys in the leg and chest, dropping him to the floor.

People were running and ducking down behind the bar and tables. Kareem ran from the bathroom when he heard the shots, gun in hand. He saw one guy still shooting at the VIP. He ran up behind him and put the Glock 40 to the back of his head and pulled the trigger. Blood went everywhere, he looked at the guy on the floor and pointed his gun at his head. Jaheem ran from the VIP to the floor where Kareem was and pointed his gun at the man's head on the floor.

"Pussy boy, you tried to kill Malachi and got yourself killed." Kareem nodded at Jaheem. Jaheem pulled the trigger, shooting him in the head twice.

"Come on, Jaheem, let's get Malachi and get the fuck up out of here." Once at the VIP booth, they helped Malachi up and ran out the back door to the club.

"Fuck naw, that nigga shot me in the shoulder, who the fuck was they?"

"Two crackers, I think they were Pete's people."

"Pete done fucked up, his shooters missed, them motherfuckers hit me but ain't kill me. I'ma show that cracker how to put blood in the streets now." Malachi was holding his wounded shoulder as Jaheem drove them out of there.

Chapter 7

"So now we have Malachi and Peter going at each other's throats?" Lee Holland walked into the room as he looked at Washington and Grunt as they sat at the table.

"I told Washington this was going to happen. It was only a matter of time. Malachi had one of Peter's guys killed in the auto parts store. Then Peter had two of his guys pull a move on Malachi. Malachi was shot Peter guys killed and here we are now" Grunt pulled his cigar after talking as he looked at Lee.

"Washington, when was the last time you talked to Malachi?"

"This morning."

"And what is he talking about?"

"Lee, the man has been shot, Peter tried to kill him. He wants blood and Peter's head gift wrapped."

"And Grunt, I'm guessing you talked to Peter?"

"Yeah, and the only thing he said was the nigga has to die."

"Malachi's mind is made up, so is Peter's. Washington, go talk with Malachi. Grunt, you go see Peter. We need to end this now before it gets out of hand."

"It's already out of hand, Lee. The best we can do now is try to negotiate between the two of them." Lee sat at the table and looked at Washington.

"Malachi drew first blood, he's the start of this."

"No, Peter moved in on his block, he was in all rights to draw first blood."

"Just go talk to him before it gets out of hand."

Washington and Grunt both nodded as they got up from the table and walked out the room.

***

Peter had his back facing to Walter and Green as he looked out the window with a glass of brandy in his hand.

"I said I wanted Malachi dead, not shot. I wanted the nigga killed and how do the story come back to me? Malachi got shot and Green's two men are dead." Peter took a sip of his brandy as he turned around and looked at Walter and Green.

"Peter, Malachi knows we are at him now, this is the time to let him know who we are."

"Walter, Green, handle it and this time don't fuck up." Peter turned around and looked at both of them.

"Why are y'all still sitting here? Got to take care of the business." Both of them got up and walked out the office, not looking back. Peter looked and saw his office phone was ringing. He walked to his desk and picked up the phone.

***

Cordial sat in his car watching the movement on the block. When his phone went off, he saw it was Kareem calling him.

"What's up, playboy?" Cordial never took his eyes off the block.

"Where you at?" Cordial took a deep breath before talking

"I'm in Ghosttown, on Popping Avenue, waiting on this nigga Mac Town so I can roll his ass."

"Shit got real last night, Cordial." Cordial sucked his teeth.

"What went down?"

"Malachi got shot two times in the shoulder."

"Nigga, what the fuck? Who got the death wish?"

"Both them niggas got rolled last night, but Peter's head is on the chopping block."

"Say less and tell Malachi take that shit like a man, niggas get shot every day, he going to live."

"Yeah, I'ma tell him, and hurry up and roll that fool so we can deal with this cracker, Peter."

"Already." Cordial hung up the phone and placed his gun on his lap as he watched the block for Mac-Town.

***

Mr. Washington walked up to the warehouse doors. Jaheem walked up to him along with Kareem as they saw him walking up.

"Gentlemen, I came to see Malachi, is he available? If so, can you let him know that I am here?"

"Mr. Washington, he is available to see you. Jaheem, watch the door. Mr. Washington, please follow me." Mr. Washington followed Kareem to Malachi's office.

Kareem knocked two times on the door before they walked in. Malachi was sitting at his desk smoking a cigar, one leg hanging off as his foot rested on the floor. His right arm was in a sling from the gunshot to his shoulder. He looked at both men coming in the office door he got up from his office desk and walked up to Mr. Washington and shook his hand.

"Malachi, thanks for seeing me."

"Anytime, Washington. Come in and have a seat and tell me, what can I do for you? Would you like a drink?"

"No, but we can share a cigar together, how's that sound?"

"Good to me." Malachi walked around to his desk, pulled out a cigar from his top right drawer and handed it to Mr. Washington.

"Malachi, I think you know why I am here." Malachi smiled when Mr. Washington said that.

"Yeah, I know, because someone wanted to put a hole in my three-thousand-dollar suit, I guess because they ain't like the color or the fabric. I don't know, or maybe they just ain't like me."

"Malachi, we don't need a war right now, you killed one of Peter's guys then had the auto parts store burnt down. He came back and shot you... you killed two of his men that night. We need to stop this now, Malachi." Mr. Washington looked at Malachi as he smoked his cigar.

"I get shot and let me guess, Lee and Grunt want me to roll over like a little dog like nothing ever happened? Look, fuck Peter, fuck Lee, fuck Grunt and fuck peace. That's what them motherfuckers would have said if my black ass would have been killed."

"Malachi, are you sure this is the road you want to go down? Because if it is, there is no turning back, just know that."

"I been walking down the wrong road all my life and I'm still here. What you can do for me is to let Peter know it's only a matter of time before his heart stops beating."

"You know, Malachi, no one is bigger than the mob, everyone wants to be the big dog. Let me break this down to you another way. Let me show you something." Mr. Washington pulled a penny out of his pocket and placed it on Malachi's desk on the edge. Malachi looked at the penny.

"This desk represents the mob, and this penny represents you. Now, I'm telling you to stand down, we will deal with Peter. Keep the penny as a reminder of where you stand."

"Is that a threat?"

"No, it's me helping you," Malachi watched as Mr. Washington got up out of the chair. He nodded at him as he walked out Malachi's office.

Once Washington was gone, Kareem walked back into the office and up to Malachi, as Malachi sat on the edge of his desk looking at the penny Mr. Washington left. He took his eyes off of the penny as he looked up at Kareem.

"How that little conversation go?" Malachi got off the desk and picked the penny up and put it in his pocket.

"I think I might be taking a trip to Queens, there's somebody I might have to have a conversation with out there." Kareem nodded.

"Just let me know when you are trying to take the trip."

"I will. Any word back from Cordial?"

"Yeah, I talked to him a little while ago. He's taken care of everything on his end."

"Good. Come on, we need to go see Jazmine and Bishop." Both men walked out the office to Malachi's limo.

***

Cordial watched as Mac-Town walked out the house, he put his hoodie on and started walking down the street. Cordial opened his car door and started walking behind him, with his gun in his hand behind his back. The block was quiet, nobody was out. Mac-Town stopped and pulled a box of Newports out of his pocket and lowered his head as he put one in his mouth and lit it. Within seconds, Cordial smacked Mac-Town in the back of the head with the gun, dropping him to the ground. Mac-Town rolled over and looked up at Cordial as he was holding his head.

"Man, who the fuck are you?" Cordial shook his head.

"The nigga who going to reunite you with your two dead homies. Y'all tried to rob my home girl, y'all shot at my homegirl and because of that, you are going to die behind my home girl."

"It wasn't me, bro, I was just getting a ride. I ain't know what them niggas was up to, I swear to God, man."

"You are who you hang with." Cordial pulled the trigger three times, killing Mac-Town. He looked at Mac-Town's dead body and walked off, leaving him dead in the street with three holes in the chest.

SAYNOMORE

36

Chapter 8

"Peter, I'm here because Lee said stand down, don't take no more shots at Malachi, your shooters missed. It's over, Peter."

"Grunt, you telling me that three of my guys get killed, my auto parts store set on fire, and Lee is telling me to stand the fuck down?"

"Yes that is what I'm telling you, stand down."

"Can you tell me why I'm standing down for a nigga who Lee don't want his blood in the streets?"

"Because you or Malachi ain't bigger than the mob and the mob come first." Peter got up from the table and walked to the window and pointed his finger out the window.

"My name holds weight and respect in these streets, and you are telling me Lee wants me to lay down for a nigga?" Grunt got up and walked to the window next to Peter.

"The same respect you get in the Bronx is the same respect we show you at the high table. So, when Lee says stand down, you stand down and when he says eat, you clean your plate. Lee ain't say eat, he said stand down. So, you stand down." Peter looked at Grunt and nodded.

"I'm glad we got a clear understanding, Peter. Now I have to go, and I will tell Lee you respected his wishes." Grunt patted Peter on the back two times before walking out of his office.

***

Malachi stepped out of the limo, along with Kareem, Bishop and Jazmine. Jaheem and Cordial stepped out of the BMW behind them.

"This is where we make our mark, I promise all of you, from this point on, we only go up. These projects are our headquarters. Let me be the first to say to all of you, welcome to Admiral Row Homes. Ya thought we were getting money before, y'all get ready for a new tax bracket, we are here now." All of them smiled as they walked into the apartments.

Chapter 9

One Year Later

"Captain Fuller, we told you a year ago this was going to happen. There are more people getting killed in Brooklyn than ever before. There is a pipeline of drugs from Brooklyn to the Bronx, to Queens, even as far as NJ and there is only one name that keeps coming up. Malachi Williams, or like we said a year ago, Mr. Untouchable."

Captain Fuller looked at Detective Benlose and detective Oldham,

"Detective Oldham, you have something you want to add on to what Detective Benlose just said?"

"We need to take Malachi down, he's bigger than Peter Drews now. Here, look at these pictures we have of Malachi." Detective Oldham passed the pictures to Captain Fuller. Captain Fuller looked at the pictures of Malachi with members of the mob, shaking their hands.

"Sir, Malachi ain't no longer a street thug, he is organized crime."

"What else do you have on him, Detective?"

"Nothing sir, but if you give us the green light we will put a case load on his ass so big it will take three D.A.'s and two judges to read over the file."

"Detective Benlose, I'ma go out on the limb for y'all, get me what the fuck I need to put this son of a bitch away."

"That's all we asked for, sir." Both detectives got up and walked out of Captain Fuller's office.

***

"Let me tell you how this works, you tell me what I need to know, or you die. Look at you, there's no way out of this for you. Where do Peter Drews keep his product at?" Rob looked up at Malachi as he was tied down to the chair, bleeding from the mouth and right eye.

"I don't know, that's above my pay grade," Rob said with short breath as he talked with broken ribs. Malachi looked at Jaheem and nodded. Jaheem took the nail gun and placed it on Rob's knee and pulled the trigger, sending a nail right through his kneecap. Rob let out a loud cry from the pain.

"Rob, I can do this all day. I don't give a fuck about your white ass, just like I know you don't give a fuck about my black ass. Me and Peter had on understanding. I stay in Brooklyn, he stays in the Bronx, and we all live happily ever after, but what do I see? You in Brooklyn making pick-ups on my blocks with these two dead motherfuckers over there. Now Peter is going to pay the fucking piper. Jaheem, kill this son of a bitch. Cut his throat from ear to ear and bury him in the field next to the pine tree."

Jaheem walked up behind Rob and pulled his knife out and cut his neck from ear to ear. Malachi looked at him then lit his cigar and nodded as he walked out of the basement to the house.

***

Peter sat in his office with his legs crossed and his finger on his head as he held a glass of Crown Royal in his hand with two ice cubes inside. He listened to Walter talk.

"Walter, let me stop you, we are talking over a million dollars in missing cocaine that Rob and Jimmy were supposed to pick-up. Not only that, the two delivery guys are missing. I talked to Calvin for over two hours over the phone. Now let me paint the picture for you. Rob and Jimmy are swimming with the fishes and so is Calvin's boys, do you get what I'm saying. They are fucking dead, and Malachi's name is written all over it."

"So, what you want me to do, boss?"

"You know what, fuck Washington, Lee and Grunt, go kill that nigga." Peter took a sip of his Crown Royal as he watched Walter leave his office. He opened up his desk drawer and pulled out his stress balls as he started thinking to himself, knowing the fire that's about to come down on New York City.

Chapter 10

"Malachi, you sure you want to do this?" Malachi looked in the mirror at his reflection as he looked at his Gucci suit.

"Kareem, my mind was made up when I walked into this store. I knew I was going to spend fourteen hundred dollars on a Salvatore Ferragamo sweater, and forty-one hundred on a pair of Gucci pants. A thousand on George Cleverley boots sixty-five hundred on my TAG Heuer watch and twenty-six hundred on my Bulgari ring. The point I'm making is that once my mind is made up, it's made up. Send Cordial to handle the business."

"You got it, Malachi, I'll get it done."

"I know you will." Kareem walked out the store, leaving Malachi and Bishop inside. Bishop walked up to Malachi,

"Malachi, I have never questioned you, but are you sure this is what you want to do?"

"Bishop, it's already done. Fuck Lee, with him out the picture, I can control Washington and if I can't, I'll kill him. What I need right now is to be more than Brooklyn but the King of New York, and if the price to pay is blood then let the bodies drop. Come on, we got somewhere to be." Malachi patted Bishop on the back as they walked out the store.

Detective Oldham and Benlose watched as Malachi and Bishop got into the LS 500 Lexus and drove off.

"Oldham, we are going to need one of Malachi's men to turn on him, that's the only way we are going to get him. He's too smart to fall for an undercover."

"Benlose, I'm afraid you're right. If I had my way, I would put a bullet into his fucking head and end all of this bullshit."

"You don't have to worry. Malachi's time is coming. You live by the gun, you die by the gun."

"Fucking right."

***

Jazmine sat at the table looking like an icon with Larry and David as she waited for Malachi and Bishop to show up. The waitress walked up to their table.

"I'm sorry for the wait, can I please take your order?" Larry looked at Jazmine.

"Jazmine, would you like to order us something to drink as we wait for Malachi to arrive?"

"Sure, I don't mind." Jazmine looked at the waitress. "Can you bring us a bottle of Laurent-Perrier on ice please, and when our other party arrives, we will order our food."

"Sure, I will be back in a few." Larry looked at Jazmine once the waitress walked off.

"That was a good choice of champagne, Cuvee Rosé. So how long have you been working for Malachi, Jazmine?"

"From the very beginning." Larry and David smiled when she said that. He knew where her loyalty was before Jazmine could say another word. The waitress walked to the table with the bottle of champagne in a basket of ice.

"When your other guests arrive, I will be back to take your orders."

"Thank you," Jazmine said.

"You're welcome." After the waitress walked off, Jazmine continued to talk.

"Larry, loyalty is more than words, it means you trust the person you are working with. And for Malachi, I will cross the Caspian Sea, walk the desert, I will be who he needs me to be. A lover, a preacher, or even a murderer." Jazmine looked at Larry and David, as she picked up her glass of champagne and took a sip, never breaking eye contact with them. David picked up his glass of champagne and tipped it towards Jazmine as he nodded his head at her and took a sip. At that time, Malachi and Bishop were walking towards them, Larry and David got up to shake their hands. Malachi looked at Jazmine, she gave him a hug and kiss on the right cheek. Then they all sat at the table together.

"Gentlemen, I apologize for my late arrival."

"No problem, Jazmine has been most entertaining. So, should we talk business, Malachi?"

"Yes, we should."

"This is what I will bring to the table for you. Protection and twenty-eight thousand a kilo, with the purchasing of a hundred or more. Can you play with them numbers?" Malachi smiled as he looked at Larry and David.

"The numbers I had in mind were more in the range of two-hundred-fifty kilos pre-shipment."

"I respect how you do business, Malachi, I see a beautiful relationship between the two of us." At that time, the waitress walked back to their private table.

"Are you ready to order now?"

"Yes, we all will take the special of the day."

"That's great, your order will be ready in twenty-five minutes." The waitress smiled as she walked away.

"Larry, how does this protection work now?"

"I have judges, D.A.'s and cops. That's the protection I can offer you."

"Good, I can always use protection." Malachi waved the waitress over and ordered a bottle of Courvoisier Cognac XO. "Larry and David, now let's drink to a beautiful relationship with something a little bit stronger."

Detectives Benlose and Oldham were three private booths back as they watched Malachi's table.

"I think we can say it now. Malachi has just become Mr. Untouchable, Oldham." Detective Oldham was taking pictures of everyone at the table.

"My question is, how did Malachi reach out to Larry Bombeno? This changes the ball game now, Benlose."

"Yeah, that's why I said he's now Mr. Untouchable, he's on a whole new level with made men."

"Come on, let's get out of here before someone sees us."

SAYNOMORE

Chapter 11

"Peter told me Malachi is behind the cocaine that's missing and our two guys. I been dealing with Peter for a very long time, I don't see any reason for him to lie. I don't know this Malachi, but I heard stories about him and at the end of the day, he's just a nigga with money to me. But I need to know if he took my shit and killed my guys… and if he did, I will have his ass skinned alive."

Calvin looked at Robert Pacino as he took a sip of his Dobel Diamante Tequila.

"I know a few people who have dealings with Malachi, let me see what I can find out. From what I'm told about him, he plays on the up and up. What I also know is that him and Peter Drews have a very bad history with each other, and it's been that way for over a year now, to where Grunt and Washington had to step in and pay both of them a visit." Robert Pacino pulled on his cigar after saying that.

"Yeah, Robert, I heard something about that." Robert got up and looked at Calvin and shook his hand.

"Calvin, I will be in touch." Calvin nodded.

"I'll be waiting to hear from you." Robert walked out of the pool hall, leaving Calvin at the back table.

***

The room was quiet as Lee paced the floor. Grunt and Washington sat in the chair looking at him as he smoked his cigar waiting for him to talk. News got back to them about Peter's men and the cocaine shipment that was taken, and how Calvin Reeves was missing and how it happened in Brooklyn. Lee stopped pacing the floor.

"Peter was wrong for doing business in Brooklyn but if Malachi had his men killed as well as Calvin Reeves' men, he crossed the line and it's time for him to be dealt with. I'm taking my gloves off. If you can't control your dog I'm putting him down."

"Brooklyn is Malachi's city. Peter crossed the line by doing business there, so whatever happened to Peter and Calvin's men was a risk they took by going to Brooklyn. Peter has the Bronx, Calvin has Queens, Robert Pacino has Manhattan and all three of us have all five Boroughs in the palms of our hands. There was no point for them to be in Brooklyn, so if you are going to take your gloves off, you need to take them off towards Peter and Calvin before you start looking at Malachi, Lee." Lee looked at Washington as he pulled his cigar.

"It's because of you, Washington, we are even having this conversation about Malachi. For the last year and a half, Malachi has killed and kidnapped, he has been extorting people. He has disrespected this table and I know he had his hands in Calvin and Peter's men being killed."

"You don't know that, Lee. Yes, everything you said about Malachi is true, from kidnapping, murder and extorting, but he did what he had to do to get the name he has. That is very respected in Brooklyn and to get a name like Malachi's the price was violence and in today's world people only respect violence Lee, I think you know that." Lee walked to the table and put his cigar out.

"You know what, Grunt, you may be right. But since you and Washington know it all, I will leave you two to deal with this mess." Lee walked out of the room, leaving them sitting at the table.

"What's your thoughts, Washington, on this whole thing?"

"Lee will never like Malachi no matter what, and he's not going to stop till Malachi is dead. Lee's mind is made up already and he's siding with Peter on this, no matter what we say to him."

"You are right about that, Washington."

"So, where do we go from here?" Grunt got up from the table and walked to the bar, poured two glasses of Whitley Neill London dry gin, and walked back to the table and handed Washington the glass.

"We drink before the storm of bullshit comes our way."

"That sounds good to me."

***

Lee walked downstairs to the parking garage. He looked at his 2021 Audi front tire and saw it was flat.

"You have to be fucking kidding me," Lee said out loud to himself. As he pulled his phone out to call AAA, that's when Cordial walked up from behind a blue Ford pick-up truck.

"No, you ain't catch a flat, I did that. I had to get you somewhere alone and dark, where you would be off guard. And what's a better place than at your own business?"

"You're on camera, nigga, someone might be looking at you right now, you won't make it out of here alive."

"Why won't I? I took the cameras down this morning, look up." Lee looked up and saw the cameras were cut down, when he looked back at Cordial, he saw the black 9mm with the silencer pointed at him.

"Malachi sent you."

"Yeah, he did." Before Lee could say another word, Cordial shot him twice in the head, killing him. He looked around before walking off with his gun in his hand.

SAYNOMORE

Chapter 12

Malachi sat in his office drinking a glass of Justin Isosceles Paso Robles as he smoked his cigar and watched the news on Lee Holland assassination.

News reporter started saying, "Yesterday at Heartbeat Inn, mob boss and drug lord Lee Holland, was assassinated in the parking garage of his industry business. He was shot two times in the head. His body was found by the security team. There are no details on whether the police have any information on the shooter at this time." Malachi cut the TV off after watching that brief newscast on Lee Holland's assassination. He sent Cordial to do a job and that's what he did, his job.

***

Robert Pacino picked up the phone and called Peter, after a few rings Peter picked up the phone.

"Peter, it's Robert. I need to ask you one question, and I just want a yes or no."

"I already know what you are going to ask me, the answer is no, I had nothing to do with it."

"So, what you are telling me is that Malachi is taking out mob bosses now?"

"I told you he was a dog off the chain. Now Lee paid the price of blood with his life for Washington's dog."

"I didn't like Lee's ways, but he was a friend of mine and we all need to have a conversation about him, meaning Malachi. I'll set something up."

"And where do you want this meeting to take place?"

"I'll call you with the details later this week."

"I'll be waiting on your call."

"Ok." Robert Pacino hung up the phone and leaned back in the chair he was seated in. He asked himself, "Could Peter have done this and just put Malachi's name on it?"

SAYNOMORE

***

"Who you think did this one, Oldham?" Detective Oldham was sitting at his desk reading over the autopsy report.

"Detective Benlose, the question we should be asking is who had enough balls to green light this hit? Fuck, who pulled the trigger? Who ordered the hit is the question. We are talking about a real made man here."

"Yeah, he had a fucked-up jacket from the age of fourteen, he started off by stealing cars. After doing fifteen months in juvenile, he was back on the streets. He started to run with a gang, they called themselves the Bronx Boys. Lee Holland graduated from stealing cars to selling drugs. After a few years, he was running his own block. At the age of twenty-one, he got locked up for murder, he shot someone in the chest and killed them. Then he beat the trial and three more trials after that, he became the head of the mob family Teliono and went on the rise from there. After ten years at age thirty-two, he got locked up for kidnapping and murder, etc. etc. Once again, he beat the trial and disappeared off the scene. He went straight for twenty years so they say, and you know the rest."

"So, let's look at the list we have to go off of, Oldham."

"I'm listening."

"Peter Drews, Calvin Reeves, Robert Pacino, Malachi Williams."

"How I knew you were going to throw that name in the bunch?"

"What, you don't think Malachi Williams had a motive to kill Lee Holland?"

"Honestly, I don't think he's that big of a shot caller yet, Benlose." Detective Benlose tapped his pen on the table when Detective Oldham said that.

"You may be right, Oldham, let's go see what the streets are talking about."

"Let's go."

***

"Washington, I want blood in the streets behind this one. I don't give a fuck who called the hit, but they crossed the fucking line." Grunt was walking the office floor talking. He had five of his bodyguards with him, standing guard.

"You are not the only one who wants blood for this, Grunt. I want blood as well, and so do Calvin Reeves and Robert Pacino. We need to know who called this hit and chop their fucking head off. As of right now, what we need to do is watch Malachi and Peter." Washington got up from his chair and walked up to Grunt and patted him on the back.

"I promise you, whoever called this hit will fucking die behind it." Washington turned around and walked to the office door with three of his personal guards with him.

As Grunt watched them walk out the door, he pulled a cigar out of his pocket, walked to the window and lit it as he looked out. of it. He watched as Washington and his men get into the car and drove off.

***

"Kareem, here comes the truck now pulling in." Kareem watched as the bread truck backed into the parking space. The back door to the truck lifted up and one of David's men jumped out, holding a bag in his hand.

"It's ballgame time, where are we unloading this at?" Kareem smiled and nodded.

"Put everything in that door over there to the right, someone already in there waiting on you." Kareem pulled his phone out and called Malachi, after a few rings Malachi picked up.

"Talk to me, Kareem, how we looking?"

"We good, everything beautiful." Malachi closed his eyes and bit down on his bottom lip.

"That's what the fuck I'm talking about. Good, keep me posted."

"Copy." Kareem hung up the phone and finished watching them unload the truck.

***

Walter walked up to Peter as he was sitting at the bar watching the boxing match. He was talking shit as he was smoking his cigar and taking shots of gin. Walter tapped him on the shoulder.

"If I'm looking at you, then you must be here to tell me Malachi is dead."

"No, we are about to take care of that now, we know where he's at, boss." Peter looked at Walter.

"I want that nigga dead and everything around him. If it breathes, it dies." Walter nodded as he went to walk off.

When Peter called him, he stopped and turned around.

"Yeah, boss?"

"I want everything fucking dead, everything." Walter didn't say anything, he just nodded and walked off. Peter turned around to finish watching the boxing match.

"You got to be fucking kidding me, I turn my head for two fucking seconds, and he gets knocked the fuck out, come on. Shit!" Peter punched the bar as he took a shot of gin.

***

Malachi was standing in front of the restaurant talking to Bishop and Casper.

"Bishop, with Lee dead, all fingers are going to point to me. They are going to come at us. I need everyone to be on point, with Larry supplying us. There is no stopping us, we go up from here."

"So, shouldn't we start shooting first? Fuck them crackers, like you said, we here now." Malachi nodded as he agreed with Bishop.

"What's your thoughts, Casper, how you feel about this shit?"

"If they not with us, fuck them. I don't give a fuck about a dead cracker."

"It's settled then, all them motherfuckers is on the plate. Let everyone know."

Malachi turned around and looked down the block and saw a blue and white ice cream truck coming down the street, he turned around to finish talking to Bishop and Casper. When Bishop turned around, he saw the guns pointed at them from the ice cream truck. Before Bishop could say a word, bullets were flying. Casper got shot in the chest and three more of Malachi's men were killed. Malachi was behind a car shooting back at the ice cream truck.

As Bishop got shot in the leg and arm, Malachi looked and saw Bishop drop to the ground. That's when the truck pulled off. Malachi ran to the middle of the street shooting at the ice cream truck as it drove off. When Malachi looked around, the restaurant windows were shot out, three of his guys were dead and two shot. Their cars were shot up and this was the second attempt on his life. Malachi was taking deep breaths as he helped Bishop and Casper up. He got them both in the car and drove off before the police came.

Chapter 13

"Malachi, I know you are upset, people hate that you have become so powerful and successful. Look how you took over Brooklyn and your name has come up in Lee's murder. You have to look at all the ins and outs that's around you. A black man that's becoming bigger than the mob, and you have people who just don't like it." Malachi looked at Larry talking as he smoked his cigar, and was throwing a baseball in his yard, playing with his dog.

"If they thought I had my hands in Lee's assassination, why didn't Washington come talk to me yet about it?" Larry looked at Malachi and stopped throwing the ball to his dog and looked at Malachi seriously.

"What makes you think they not talking about it behind your back? You need to ask yourself Malachi, would they do it? Does Washington really have your back?" Malachi thought about what Larry said for a second.

"Malachi, let me tell you this. If Washington comes to talk to you about setting up a meeting, he has already agreed to set you up to be killed. Don't trust him. Whoever comes to set the meeting up is setting you up."

"Your word to me was that I would be protected, this don't feel like I'm protected, Larry."

"I did promise you protection, against the law, not the mob. You and I both know what you need to do. Cut the head off and let the body fall." Malachi nodded and walked off with his mind made up on what he needed to do.

***

"It's no secret why we are all here right now. Lee's murder will not go unanswered and the one name that keeps coming up is Malachi. Do I think he had Lee killed? I don't know, for all we know Peter had Lee killed but what we do know is that Lee is dead and somebody has Lee's blood on their hands."

Calvin Reeves looked at Robert, Washington, Grunt, and a few other people sitting at the table.

"Malachi thinks he is bigger than the men at this table, he thinks he is bigger than the mob. Peter's family has been a part of this table for over forty years. Never in the history of the mob have we ever had to answer to a black man, fuck it, a nigga. I say we kill Malachi, and we all take a part of Brooklyn."

Calvin sat down at the table after saying that. Grunt stood up and looked at everyone.

"I never liked Malachi, but I respected him because of Washington, do I think Malachi has Lee's blood on his hand? Yes, I do. Everyone knows at this table that Peter ain't like Lee and Lee ain't like Peter, but they respected each other. Both of them are made men and you don't kill a made man. Washington, you told Malachi to stand down on the auto parts store on 114th Street. What did he do? He still killed Peter's men and set the place to flames, he has no respect for higher ranks. I vote we kill the nigga." Grunt sat down after saying what he said. Everyone looked at Washington. Washington stood up.

"No one is bigger than the mob. Malachi is not a part of the mob and that's a fact. But this is what I will say about him, he turned Brooklyn into a gold mine. Let's face the facts. This is bigger than Lee's murder. This is about Brooklyn and Lee's murder was just the spark that started the fire. Yes, I told Malachi to stand down and he didn't. Do I think he had his hands in Lee's murder? I don't know but I'm leaning towards yes, because of his actions in the past. I'm not bigger than the mob, so whatever y'all vote on today I will stand with it." Washington sat down after saying that.

Robert Pacino stood up.

"I vote, kill Malachi and sanction Peter to stay out of Brooklyn, and one-million-five dollars for the unsuccessful hit on Malachi that Lee told him not to do. We at this table have the power to vote on his death. However, Larry is the senior who can call this off. But he's not here, so again my vote is kill Malachi and sanction Peter. Who stands with me?" Robert looked around at everyone, one by one they all raised their hands.

"It stands then, Malachi must die," Robert said.

"Washington, Malachi trusts you, so you must be the one who sets him up to get killed." Grunt said.

Washington just nodded.

SAYNOMORE

Chapter 14

"Loyalty has a different meaning for some people. I'm walking around this junkyard with you, as you tell me how Peter was the one who tried to kill me, shot two of my guys and killed three of them. All for two hundred thousand dollars, Tony." Tony looked at Malachi as they walked, and Malachi's guards drove the SUV behind them watching his every move.

"Fuck loyalty. Loyalty gets you killed or life in prison. I'm in this to win." Malachi nodded.

"Understood. So, what else do you have to tell me, Tony?"

"They all plan on killing you. They had a meeting the other night." Malachi stopped and looked at Tony.

"Who had a meeting?" Tony pulled out a pack of Camels and lit one and let out the smoke before talking again.

"Washington, Grunt, Calvin Reeves, Robert Pacino, Frank, Lil John, and a few other people. They voted to kill you."

Malachi placed his hand on Tony's shoulder and looked into his eyes.

"Thank you, Tony, everything you came forward and told me really helped me today." Malachi waved to Jaheem. Jaheem stepped out of the SUV with a black bag in his hand and walked towards them.

"Tony, the money is in the bag." After Malachi said that he walked off to the SUV. Jaheem walked past Malachi up to Tony and handed him the black bag. Tony took the bag and looked inside. While he was looking at the money inside the bag, Jaheem pulled the black 9mm out and shot Tony two times in the head, killing him. Malachi was in the SUV watching everything unfold. Jaheem turned around and walked back to the SUV. Once inside, he looked at Malachi.

"If he came to you with information, why you kill him?" Malachi cut his eyes at Jaheem.

"One, because he made it very clear he has no loyalty. And two, if he ain't have no loyalty for his crew, why would he give two fucks about us?"

Jaheem nodded.

"What about the money?"

"It's his blood money, let him keep it," Jaheem ain't say a word as he drove off, leaving Tony dead with his head laying on a book bag filled with money.

***

Walking into Peter's office, Walter didn't say a word. He took his seat in the front of Peter's desk as he talked over the phone. Peter just looked at Walter.

"Are you sure? Ok, thanks for the call and thanks for cleaning it up for me. I owe you one." Peter hung up the phone and lit his cigar.

"Everything's alright, boss?"

"That was Little John, he said they just found Tony's body in the junkyard. He was shot two times in the head and his head was laying on a bag of money."

"You have to be fucking kidding me. Are they sure it was Tony?" Peter pulled his cigar before talking.

"Yeah, they are sure."

"You think it was Malachi?"

"I don't think, I know it was him."

"You want me to take care of this?"

"Yeah, let's show New York City a war like they have never seen before. Anyone who is working with Malachi, I want them dead."

"You got it, Peter." Walter got up and walked out of Peter's office with a smile on his face.

Chapter 15

Captain Fuller looked at Detectives Oldham and Benlose, as the chief of police and District Attorney Cox all sat in the office.

"There is no other way to put this, we have a war on our hands. Every time I turn around there are shootings, car bombings, killings, people getting found in the East River, under bridges and in the trunk of cars. We are losing our grip on New York City to organized crime. This is a war we cannot afford to lose. It makes all of us look bad." District Attorney Cox sat down after he said what he said.

"A little over a year ago, we told all of you in this room that Malachi Williams was becoming the untouchable, to where the mob wants him dead, and he is putting up a helluva fight against them. We have nothing on Malachi Williams but some pictures of him talking to other members of the mob. To get Malachi, we need someone in his crew to turn on him. That knows about the murders, drug deals, and people he is connected to. That's the only way we are going to get to him." Detective Oldham looked around after he said that.

"Malachi has a loyal crew, so we might need someone to go undercover. That might be the only way to get him." Captain Fuller took a sip of water after he made that statement. All eyes were on him. Detective Benlose shook his head. Captain Fuller looked at him.

"Detective, is there something you want to say?"

"Yeah, there is, Captain. If we put an undercover in there, there's going to be one or two outcomes. One, that undercover agent is going to become a murder or two, someone will be at the station to ID his body. The only shot me and Detective Oldham got to get in with Malachi is to kill someone in front of him. You don't know when it's gone be or where, but if you don't, you die. If we put someone in there, all we are doing is setting him up to fail. He's gone to have a choice, kill or be killed. Like Detective Benlose said, we need someone in his crew to turn against him that's the only way. We need the weak link."

"Ok, let's get off of Malachi for a minute, what about Peter Drews? Can we get him?"

District Attorney Cox stood up after the chief said that.

"No, we went after him too many times and in the end, he beat every case and won two lawsuits. The best way to end this war is to get the small fish in the lake and that's Malachi Williams." Captain Fuller looked at both detectives.

"So, the question we need to know is, what do y'all need to bring his ass down?" Detective Benlose and Oldham looked at each other.

"A loyal team of five men that's ready to get their hands dirty, and I promise you we will bring that son of a bitch down, sir" Captain Fuller looked at D.A. Cox and the chief of police after Detective Benlose said that. The chief of police nodded at him, so did D.A. Cox.

"Detective, you got your team, now let's nail this son of a bitch to the cross."

"That's all we needed to hear, sir." Both detectives got up and walked out of the meeting.

***

Malachi looked out of the window, as the black limo pulled up and Washington stepped out of it. He had six of his men in front of his place of business. Kareem walked Washington to Malachi's office. Malachi just looked at him.

"Malachi, let's share a drink instead of a cigar this time. How's that sound?"

"It sounds good to me." Malachi walked to the bar and poured himself and Washington some silver Patrón tequila edicion limitada. He walked up to Washington and handed him the glass. They tapped glasses and took their seats.

"Malachi, I think you know why I'm here. There is so much bloodshed in the streets right now, everyone is losing money. We have the police cracking down on us, families are going under investigation, everyone is losing right now. Bottom line, this war needs to end right now." Malachi didn't say a word, he just took a sip of his drink and remembered what Larry told him. *Whoever comes to set the meeting up is the one setting you up to be killed.*

"So, what do you have in mind then, Washington? I'm open to hear all suggestions, talk to me." Washington took another sip of his drink and placed his glass on the table.

"I think you and Peter need to have a meeting and I can set it up for the both of you. I think that will be best for everyone." Malachi cut his eyes at Kareem, standing behind Washington by the door.

"Washington, you remember you gave me this penny a year ago and told me where I stood and where the mob stood? And I asked you was that a threat and you said, 'No, it's me helping you," before you walked out them doors right behind you?"

"Yeah, I remember every word, I see you still have the penny."

"Yeah, I do, you know why? Let me tell you. This penny taught me one thing, never put too much trust in friends and learn how to use enemies. See, I don't give two fucks about a meeting with Peter… but let me tell you this. When I strike the shepherd, the sheep will scattered." Malachi nodded at Kareem. Before Washington knew it, there was a metal wire around his neck, choking the life out of him, his face was turning blue. Malachi grabbed his hands and looked in his eyes.

"You fat fuck, you didn't think I knew you was setting me up? Now look at you. I'ma send your fucking head back to Grunt, with a note stuffed in your fucking mouth on your fat fucking tongue."

Malachi pulled his knife out of his pocket, cut Washington's throat and watched him bleed out in the chair. He took a rag and wiped the blood off his knife and put it back in his pocket.

"Kareem, go kill his driver then dump this fat fuck's body off in the East River and send his head back to Grunt." Kareem nodded and walked off. Malachi sat at the table and sipped his Patrón and looked at Washington's dead body.

SAYNOMORE

Chapter 16

"You see him?" Alexis watched Malachi walk out of the restaurant with Jazmine and get into the limo.

"Yeah, I do, Adam. He got into the limo with the female known as Jazmine, he has two cars with him. One in the front and the other behind him. That's his security team." Adam called Detective Benlose, after a few rings he picked up.

"Talk to me, Adam, what you got for me?"

"Malachi in a black limo with two car details, one in the front, the other in the back. As I know right now, the only other person in the limo with him is Jazmine."

"Which way is he headed?"

"He's going down Lincoln Avenue right now."

"Ok you and Alexis keep an eye out on the restaurant.

"Me and Detective Oldman are going to follow Malachi to see where he's going, and Lauren and Jonah are watching Admiral's Row Projects to see all activity that comes in and out of there. I'll keep you posted on who Malachi is meeting up with."

"Ten-four." Detective Benlose hung up the phone.

"That's them a few cars up… black limo, gray Lexus LS 500 in front of them, and white Audi behind them. Where do you think they are going?"

"I don't know but we are about to find out."

***

Calvin Reeves was watching the news at his bar when he saw breaking news and the reporter pointed towards the East River.

The reporter started speaking. "Today around 4:30 pm, New York City Police pulled two bodies out of the East River. One was missing its head. I was told the body missing its head was Andrew Washington, former mob boss. New York City Police are not sure how long his body's been in the East River, or who killed him." Calvin couldn't believe what he was seeing and hearing. Washington's dead, even worse, beheaded. He pulled out his phone and called Lil John, within a few seconds Lil John was on the other end of the phone.

"John, did you see the news?"

"I seen it. I still can't believe it, but I know who is behind it and I think you do too."

"The son of a bitch cut his head off and dumped his body in the river like he was trash."

"Let me make a few calls, Calvin. I think I know somebody who can take care of this for us."

"I'll be waiting to hear back from you." Calvin hung up the phone and finished watching the news.

***

"Grunt, you are the last man standing. There's a number and time limit on your name. Nobody is talking and now I'm thinking harder. Malachi don't have the manpower to do the shit that's going down. I think someone is framing him, and to do what they need to do, they need the three of you out the way. First Lee, now Washington... your day and hour is at hand if we don't put this shit together fast." Grunt looked at Robert Pacino because he had a feeling he was right.

"So, who do you have in mind?"

"Peter, Calvin, Lil John, Frank, because you don't think it's this nigga, so who?"

"I don't fucking know but we need to find out ASAP."

Grunt turned around and nodded as he lit his cigar.

***

Detective Benlose pulled up on the private road as Malachi pulled up at the lake, where Larry and David were waiting on him.

"Oldham, you seeing this?"

"Yeah, Benlose, I see Malachi got him a new best friend." Malachi walked up to Larry and David and shook their hands as Cordial and Jaheem watched everything. His other two guards stood guard. Jazmine walked up to both men and kissed them on the cheek.

"Malachi, I see Washington's body was in the East River. I asked myself, did you have something to do with that?"

"Let's just say someone came to talk to me about a meeting, then went for a swim afterwards."

"I can understand a swim, but the missing head part I'm a little bit confused on."

"You know there is all kinds of shit in the East River."

"You are right about that one. Come walk with me by the lake. I'm sure David could keep Jazmine company for a few minutes." Malachi looked at Jazmine and winked at her as he walked off.

"If I give you the keys to the city, are you strong enough to hold it down? Are you willing to cross a line that there is no coming back from?"

"If you give me the keys to the city, every door I open, I'll make sure it don't close and every line I cross, I won't look back on." Larry nodded.

"Good, because everybody in your crew has a part to play now, because I just opened the doors to the city and gave you the keys."

"So, where do we go from here?"

"You have more unfinished business to take care of, Malachi."

"And what business is that?"

"The last time I looked, Grunt was still alive. Eat your food and clean your plate, then come get your keys to the city from me." Malachi nodded.

"There's one more thing, Malachi."

"And what's that?"

"You're in the big league now, you have forty-eight hours to take care of the business."

"The job will get done before the deadline."

"Good, now let's go back to our friends, every conversation ain't for everybody ears." Larry placed his hand on Malachi's shoulder as they walked back to their cars. He looked at Jazmine and smiled.

"Jazmine, it's good to see you again."

"Likewise, Larry." Jazmine walked up to Larry and gave him a hug and a kiss on the right cheek. Malachi nodded at both men before walking back to the limo.

"Within forty-eight hours, Grunt will be dead, and Malachi will be on his way to becoming the King of New York. And just like that, David, the three wise men became the three dead men."

"I hear you, Larry, but don't forget you still have a few big hittas out there who just won't lay down."

"They can get down and respect New York City's new order, or they can lay down in their own blood and be covered with dirt."

"Let see how this plays out, Larry."

"We will, David, we will."

Detective Benlose was taking pictures of everything, as well as Detective Oldham, as they laid in the grass on the hill between the trees.

"What you think this meeting was about, Oldham?"

"Larry and David know how to move, look at where we are, an hour out of the city in the woods on a dirt road. This meeting was about a hit. Somebody is going to die, and Malachi was just given the job. And whatever Larry promised him it comes with money, power, and respect. Come on, let's get up out of here."

"Right behind you." Detective Benlose looked at the cars as they drove off, knowing something big was about to go down.

Chapter 17

Malachi walked in the room. He looked in the faces of everyone there as they sat at the table. All eyes were on him. He walked to the bar and poured himself something to drink before he started to talk.

"New York City has a new king and I'm wearing the fucking crown. There are going to be new rules, but what I need to tell you right now is that we don't have to be feared to be respected. Yes, motherfuckers respect violence, but they also respect honor. I heard niggas say you can't get money with the murders and bodies dropping. The nigga who said that is a joke to me, because we are getting money with the murders and bodies we are laying down.

"If a nigga cross the line, line them up. As a family we have to stick together, we can never have drama between each other. We are known as killers on the streets, on these blocks we own. You know why? Because we respect the game, and motherfuckers know that. They also know disrespect will get them killed. We know at this table ratting is never an option, that's why we are still here." Malachi put both hands on the table and leaned forward and looked at everyone.

"I was given the chance to have the keys to the city, we just have to pop the bottle one good time, and New York City is ours."

"Malachi, I hear what you are saying, but we still have Peter, Lil John, Calvin Reeves, Robert Pacino and a whole lot of other motherfuckers out there. And don't forget you still have Grunt calling the shots." Malachi lowered his head as he lit his cigar and looked at Kareem as he was talking.

"Kareem, we are going to strike the shepherd and the sheep will scatter. When we strike this motherfucker, we are going to do it loud, in public. You know, I never got word back about Washington's head being found. Cordial, why is that?"

"Damn, I forgot about that shit. I got it in the freezer. Where do you want me to send it? And who is this shepherd we are about to strike?" Malachi smiled.

"The last of the three wise men, and we will leave Washington's head with Grunt." Malachi licked his lips and pulled his cigar as he looked at everybody.

***

"What I'm telling y'all in this room is, something big is about to go down and Malachi's name is going to be written on it." Detective Benlose looked at D.A. Cox and Captain Fuller and the chief of police.

"Why do you think something big is about to go down, Detective Benlose?" Detective Benlose looked at Detective Oldham and nodded at him. Detective Oldham passed the folder to D.A. Cox to look at the pictures inside after that statement.

"When was this meeting?"

"Two days ago, and they ain't want nobody to know about it."

"Captain, what do you have to say about this?" Captain Fuller looked at the pictures before talking.

"Malachi has been shaking trees that no one else had the balls to. He's getting the attention from the mob. He is showing them what a pawn can do to a king."

"No, Captain, a year ago Malachi was a pawn. There were more than two kings on the chess board, and Malachi is one of them." Everyone looked at Detective Oldham when he said that because the cold fact was, they knew he was right. Malachi has become the untouchable.

"Mr. Cox, Chief, Captain, we are all in this room because we are fighting for what Brooklyn couldn't. We are fighting for peace, justice, and monsters like Malachi to be put in prison."

"Detective Benlose, we understand and hear what you are saying." Detective Benlose took a deep breath.

"Do you, Chief? Because if you did, you'd know Chief would look someone like Malachi up. You have to find someone with a heart like Malachi, that's willing to go to the limit like Malachi. And a D.A. that's willing to break the rules like Malachi, because we all are doing this for Brooklyn, and Malachi is about to be the king she'll marry." Chief Ward looked at D.A. Cox, then Captain Fuller.

"Detective... let's get Malachi in the act. I'll have a team on standby twenty-four hours a day just for this."

"Thanks, Chief." Both detectives left the room.

"D.A. Cox, if we get him, we need you to nail his ass to the cross."

"Get him and I'll handle the rest."

SAYNOMORE

72

Chapter 18

Kareem and Jazmine were watching Main Street from the third floor of the office building, while Cordial, Jaheem, and Bishop were on Main Street. Each of them was on different sides of the street, waiting for Grunt to come out of the office building. Casper was in a black tow truck across the street in the parking garage. It was 2:00 pm on the head. All eyes were on the Glamour Office Building. The doors opened and Jolivet's Grunt came walking out with four of his bodyguards walking him to the limo parked in front of the building.

Casper started up the tow truck and came out of the parking garage doing 60 mph, as Grunt and his men were getting into the limo, he closed the door to the limo. His bodyguards looked and saw the tow truck headed right at them. He was so focused on the tow truck, and he didn't see Jaheem coming from the side with the gun pointed right at his head. Jazmine took a few steps closer to the window on the third floor as Jaheem pulled the trigger, blowing one of the bodyguard's heads off. She watched as his body hit the ground. Grunt looked to see what was going on.

At that time the tow truck hit the limo with an impact so hard, it made the limo flip over on its roof, crashing into the building. Cordial and Bishop ran up with AR-15's and started shooting the limo up with Grunt and his bodyguards inside. Casper jumped out of the tow truck and started shooting up the front of the office building as more guards tried to run out. Kareem stood there quietly watching everything with his hands behind his back.

Cordial opened the limo door and pulled one of the bodyguards out and shot him two times in the head. He then pulled Grunt out. People couldn't believe what they were seeing. Grunt looked up at Cordial, but he didn't know who it was, because he had a wolf mask over his face. Cordial took two steps back as Grunt was on his hands and knees. Jaheem threw Washington's head in front of Grunt. Grunt looked at Washington's head as Bishop ran full force with a machete in his hand. With one mighty swing, Grunt's head was right next to Washington.

As his body poured out blood, Casper ran up to his body with the AR-15 and started shooting it up. Everyone looked at each other when they heard the police coming. Before they knew it, shots were coming their way and Jaheem got shot in the back and blood hit the side of the tow truck. Cordial and Bishop started shooting at the police cars, hitting both cars stopping them as Casper got Jaheem out of there. Everyone was gone before backup arrived. Kareem and Jazmine looked at each other before they walked off. Malachi wanted them to watch the whole thing to make sure it was done right.

***

Captain Fuller looked around as he walked on the scene, Main Street looked like a part of the cold war. A limo flipped over, dead bodies in the streets. He couldn't believe what he was seeing.

"Captain Fuller, Detectives Benlose and Oldham said something big was about to go down and Malachi's hands was going to be written all over it. Jolivet Grunt's head is laying on the ground, next to Andrew Washington's head. We have a dead officer down the block, a limo flipped over all on Main Street, a building shot up and nobody's seen no one's face because they all had on masks."

"Chief, I had both detectives watching Malachi all day, he hasn't left the apartment."

"He don't have to. He just had to make one call and that's all. Get both detectives down here now."

"They are already on their way, sir."

"I can't wait to see the headlines on tomorrow's newspaper about this." Chief Ward walked off, not saying another word.

***

"On Main Street at 2:00 pm, an all-out shootout, with four men wearing white masks of a wolf, bear, cat and dog we were told, took place. This was a hit on Jolivet Grunt. He was shot multiple times and his head was amputated, lying next to the missing head of Andrew Washington. This was a message to someone, but who is the question?" the news reporter said. Larry cut the TV off and picked up his phone and made a call. After a few seconds, David picked up on the other end.

"Larry, I saw the news. I'm still watching it as we speak."

"I'm glad you are seeing it, because Malachi just got the keys to the city." Larry hung up the phone with no more words to be said.

SAYNOMORE

Chapter 19

"New York City has a new king, and his name is Malachi Williams. I can't believe this shit, look, his face is on the cover of *GQ Magazine*. In the papers, they are calling him New York City's king, man of the year. What the fuck?" Captain Fuller slammed the newspaper on his desk and looked at Detectives Benlose and Oldham.

"God, please put your hand on this case and help me get this son of a bitch." At that time, there was a knock at the captain's office door.

"Come in." Captain Fuller looked at Officer Latoya from CSI, who walked in the office holding a file in her hand.

"Sir, I have good news." Captain Fuller slammed his hand on the desk and took a deep breath.

"Thank God. What you got for me?"

"I have blood for you."

"What you mean, you have blood for me?"

"There was blood on the tow truck, and it belongs to Seth Pittman. Here are the pictures of him, sir."

"This is the best news I got since the start of this investigation."

"Captain Fuller looked at the pictures of Seth Pittman, aka Jaheem.

"Detective, we got this son of a bitch. Can y'all make him roll on Malachi?"

"Do a pig play in shit?"

"Yeah, he do, Oldham."

"We have to pick him up without nobody knowing we got him."

"Just get it done. God, answer my prayers."

***

Jaheem came walking out the deli, eating a bag of chips, when Detective Oldham walked up on him and put his gun to his head.

"Behind door number one, you coming with us." Jaheem looked and saw Detective Benlose coming with his gun out.

"And behind door number two, you fucking die right here. What is it going to be?" Jaheem put his hands in the air as they took his gun from him and walked him to the undercover van, where Agents Alexis and Adam were waiting on them. Within twenty minutes, they were at a safe house outside of Brooklyn. Jaheem sat in a chair as Detective Oldham read over his case file to him, while everybody stood around and watched.

"Seth, I'ma tell you what I want, but first I'ma tell you what I'ma give you. I'ma give you a new life, a new name with a clean plate. Or you could take the second option, which is an eight by ten cell and a waiting list to put a needle in your arm. See, we have you for the murders of Andrew Washington, Jolivet Grunt, and one of our police officers. With a gun in your possession and your blood was on the scene. So, the one question is, do you stay loyal to Malachi Williams and die? Or do you live with a new beginning and a new name? The clock is ticking and the choice is yours, what's it's going to be, Seth?"

"I want everything in writing, stamped by the D.A.'s office, signed off by the judge with an attorney to verify. Then we can talk, and I'll give you everything you need to know on Malachi Williams."

Detective Oldham looked at Detective Benlose and nodded.

"Done."

Chapter 20

Detectives Benlose and Oldham, it's been two weeks, tell me what you have now that you got one of Malachi's men to turn on him." Detective Benlose got up and walked to the board he put up in the briefing room and looked back at the captain, chief, and D.A. Cox.

"For starters, we have already unburied three bodies, he also gave us the location to his main drug house. Now, the apartments Malachi owns is a front. Malachi is smart, he don't have no drugs running out of these apartments at all. Everything is on the up and up, he is using government funds to run it for low-income families, Section 8, etc. etc. Malachi never leaves this apartment. The apartment is his office. He has his own security booths there, in all it's four of them." D.A. Cox looked at Detective Benlose.

"Detective, where was these bodies unburied at? And what can you tell us about his team?"

"Jazmine, she is deadly, and she is his personal accountant. She handles all the money for Malachi. Kareem is his number-two. If you ain't one of the six, you don't talk to Malachi, you talk to Kareem. Cordial - hit man, he's the one who killed Lee. Then you have Casper - hit man. Bishop - drug dealer, and like I said earlier, Jazmine and Kareem. And you already know about Jaheem. And the three bodies were in the field by the high school. Here, I have pictures of everything."

Detective Benlose handed the pictures to D.A. Cox.

"Detective, we need to hit his drug house, pin these bodies on Malachi."

"That's not a problem, Jaheem is willing to go against Malachi, he knew it's part of his deal."

"Good, let's get this son of a bitch now."

SAYNOMORE

Chapter 21

Peter, Lil John, Calvin, Robert and Frankie all sat in the private room, as Larry and David walked the floor as Larry talked.

"This is the first time in many years me and David have had to have a meeting with the families. There's been bodies floating in the East River, car bombs, drive-bys, bodies being found in trash dumpsters, kidnappings. I'm down here now to say right now, this war is over. Washington, Lee, and Grunt is fucking dead and nobody knows who killed them, but y'all are trying to put this off on one nigga, that did to Brooklyn what no one in this room could.

"He made the bitch into a gold mine, and that's what the blood in the streets are about right now. So, we have the police, the district attorney's office, the FBI, and DEA watching us over three dead motherfuckers who ain't give two fucks about none of us. We are all men of power in this room. This business about Malachi is over. The next person to call a hit on him, will have a contract called on them. I don't need nobody to say nothing, this meeting is over." Larry nodded at David and they both walked out the room.

***

"Don't stop, go all the way down, baby, hold my balls while you suck this dick." Malachi had his eyes closed as Angel sucked on him. She stopped sucking on his wood and ran her tongue all over his abs, up to his chest, where she spelled his name on his chest with her tongue.

"Malachi, I want you to bend me over and fuck me till I cream all over this fat dick of yours, daddy." Malachi opened his eyes and looked at Angel. Angel was bad. She was dark-skinned, with a body like J-Lo, dark brown eyes and long locs that were red at the tip, a white smile with dimples. Malachi grabbed her by the waist and pulled her to the edge of the bed.

"I'm break your box long-dick style, that's what you want, right?"

"Yes, daddy." Malachi slid his thick nine and a half inches inside of Angel. Angel let out a soft moan as Malachi put himself inside her and started pumping in and out of her, harder and harder. She grabbed the bed covers and held it tight as she bit down on the pillow.

"Daddy, you are busting me open, I can feel you in my stomach. Damn, I'm about to come on this dick. I'm coming, daddy, oh God, I'm cumming." Malachi kept on pumping till he came deep inside of Angel. He looked at his dick and smiled when he saw how Angel creamed all over him.

"Daddy, I felt you cumming deep inside of me."

"Baby, that pussy is water, on God it is." Malachi kissed her, got up off the bed and walked to the shower. He let the water run down his neck and as he held the walls, he went into deep thought. He had so much more to do and right now his team was winning. He had New York and everybody knew it. He showed the mob that a pawn can turn into a king.

Chapter 22

"Don't nobody move, NYPD, freeze."

Bishop looked at the SWAT team running into the dope house. He pulled his gun out and started shooting at them as they were running in the house. He took off down the hall and picked up the two duffle bags that were on the floor and threw them out the window. He jumped out the window behind them. As he got in the car, the SWAT team was shooting at the car as he drove off.

"Detective Benlose, come look at this." Detective Benlose walked in the room where Detective Oldham was.

"What you got, Oldham?"

"Everything." When Detective Benlose looked, he saw four tables filled with bricks of cocaine, three dead females killed in the shootout, and two that was on their stomachs, cuffed up.

"We hit the fucking jackpot on this one." At that time, one of the SWAT team officers walked in the room.

"Detective, the one that was shooting, jumped out the window. He got into a black BMW and got away, but we did put out an APB out on the car."

"Fuck!" Detective Benlose said. He looked at the handcuffed female being walked out the door and stopped the officers.

"Who was that who jumped out the window?" The female looked at him, then the officer, then back at Benlose and spit in his face. The officer threw her into the wall. Benlose looked at the officer.

"Get her the fuck out of here now!"

The officer took her out the door as she yelled. "I ain't no fucking rat."

Detective Oldham walked up to Detective Benlose and handed him a rag to wipe his face.

"Come on, Benlose, let's check on Agent Alexis and them to see how they doing."

"Go ahead and make the call, Oldham." Detective Oldham pulled out his phone and called Agent Alexis. After a few rings, she picked up the phone.

"Alexis, this is Oldham, what's your location?"

"We pulling up at the apartment right now."

"Ten-four, keep me posted on everything."

"Will do, sir." Oldham hung up the phone and looked at Benlose.

"They are at the apartment now."

"Good, let's go."

"After you."

***

Kareem walked into Malachi's office. Malachi noticed the look on his face.

"Kareem what's up?"

"I just got a call from Bishop, the police just hit the dope spot." Malachi looked at him then Jazmine.

"How the fuck did they know about that spot?" Jazmine looked at the security camera and cut Malachi off from talking.

"Malachi, come look at this, we have twenty officers walking through the doors now." Malachi walked to the security cameras and looked.

"They are coming here for me. Kareem and Jazmine, y'all get out of here. I'm the only one they want, plus I need both of y'all to run shit till I get out. Jazmine, you are number one, Kareem number two. Now, both of y'all go out the back door now." Malachi pulled out a Cuban cigar and lit it, then walked to his bar and poured himself a shot of Courvoisier cognac XO. He was sitting on the edge of the table when the police opened his office door. He looked at them and smiled.

"New York's Finest, welcome to Admiral's Row. Now tell me, what can I do for you?" Malachi took his shot and pulled his cigar after he said that. Agent Alexis walked up to him with an arrest warrant.

"Malachi Williams, you are under arrest for murder, kidnapping, aggravated assault, extortion and organized crime." Malachi smiled as he pulled his cigar.

"Is that all?" Malachi put his cigar in the ashtray on the table and got up and placed his hands behind his back as Agent Alexis handcuffed him and walked him out the office.

***

"This is Kaya Stone with *Channel 5 News*. Drug lord Malachi Williams has been arrested for murder, kidnapping, aggravated assault, extortion and organized crime. Malachi Williams has been shaking trees in Brooklyn that no one else could, he was a pawn that turned into a king. New York Police have been trying to get something on Malachi Williams for the last two years. He is being charged with the multiple bodies found in the East River, car bombs, and drive-by shootings. We are being told the district attorney's office has a cooperating witness against Malachi Williams, who is willing to testify against him. Keep your station here on *Channel 5 News* for more updates."

Kareem looked at Jazmine and Bishop.

"Jaheem is a fucking rat. He told everything. I talked to Malachi's attorney yesterday and he is asking for bail. But he is not sure he will be given one. Malachi has a hard ass district attorney named Cox who got it out for him." Jazmine shook her head.

"I'ma kill that son of a bitch Jaheem."

"Jazmine, relax, Malachi don't want nothing done to him yet. Plus, we don't know if this place is bugged or not. Bishop, what all did they get out the spot?"

"Just two hundred kilos. I got the money and got up out of there."

"Good, everything goes on pause till I hear from Malachi. Stay low and out the way, but we need to find out where they are keeping Jaheem, so everybody get on that. But nobody pushes the button till we hear from Malachi, understood?" Jazmine and Bishop nodded.

SAYNOMORE

Chapter 23

Present Day

"Malachi Williams is looking at three life sentences, plus four-hundred-twenty years. With this nigger out the way, I'll move in on Brooklyn and take over. Who would think one of his own men would be the one to turn on him? I told you, Walter, niggers ain't loyal at all. That's why I would never do business with one of them." Peter smiled as he read the newspaper and smoked his cigar in his office.

"You know what gets me, boss?" Peter looked at Walter and placed the newspaper down on his desk.

"No, tell me what gets you, I'm all ears."

"Malachi is being charged with multiple murders and it just came out that he is the one who had Lee, Grunt and Washington knocked off, and Larry and David don't want him touched. When did the mob start letting niggas knock off mob bosses?" Peter pulled his cigar and looked at Walter and pointed his finger at him.

"You make a damn good point, something just ain't adding up now that I think about it."

"I'm just saying, boss, I think we should look into it."

"You are right, let me make a call." Peter picked up the phone and called an old friend of his, while Walter read the newspaper that was on his desk.

***

"Malachi, I know you are worried about this trial. You are looking at a lot of time in prison, but like I told you before when you shook my hand, and we made that deal a little over a year ago. I told you I will protect you. Well, that's what I'm doing. How do you think you were able to get out on bond? It wasn't that high priced attorney. Just put a story together and make it sound good."

Malachi picked up his drink and took a sip as Larry was talking to him on the deck of his yacht.

"The witness, I need to know where I can find him at? Can you get me an address for him?"

"That's something I can work on, but I can't make no promises on that. He is the district attorney's golden boy. My people don't even know where this bull D.A. Cox got him at." Larry pulled his cigar as he threw the yacht in drive.

"Look, don't worry about the case. It's already beat, they can't link you to no crimes. My judge already told me that you are going to walk." Malachi nodded.

"Now, come on, it's a beautiful day let's do a little fishing while the sun is up. And remember, Malachi, we are all pawns serving the same king. The almighty dollar."

***

"It's been a long time since we been down this road together. Fifteen or twenty years, Robert?"

"It's been many years, Peter, many. So, what is it that you wanted to talk to me about?"

"Lee, Grunt, and Washington. A lot of things just ain't adding up."

"Like what?"

"Let's put it all out on the table, we all know that Malachi is the one who had them killed, but Larry and David won't let nobody touch him, why?"

"Let's cut through the chase, you are thinking Larry Green lighted it, that's why Malachi did it?"

"Bingo, you said it on the head."

"But why would Larry do that? That's the question you need to ask yourself."

"I already did, with them out the way and Malachi selling his drugs in all five boroughs, who could stop him?"

"But Malachi only has Brooklyn and he's not going to sell outside of Brooklyn."

"You make a good point, but that don't mean them niggas won't come to Brooklyn to shop with him and then go back to Queens, the

Bronx, or wherever they come from. Malachi still gets his money and so do Larry and David's ass."

"You said a mouthful just now, Peter. We need to look into that and if you are right, Larry and David will be taking a swim with the fishes."

"And that's my point." Both of them shook hands before going back to their cars and driving off.

SAYNOMORE

Chapter 24

As Malachi sat in the courtroom, District Attorney Cox made him look like a monster to the people of the court and jury, showing them pictures of dead victims as he pointed his finger at Malachi.

"New York City Police have been pulling bodies out of the East River for the last year. The last victim was beheaded when the New York City Police Department pulled his body out of the river. Mothers, fathers, brothers, sisters, sons, and daughters were being killed every day by the order of Malachi Williams. Malachi Williams has been putting drugs on the streets of New York City for years, he is the reason the crime rate is so high, from murder to kidnapping to extortion. He has organized crime in New York."

Malachi smiled as D.A. Cox painted a picture of him. They both caught eye contact with each other, D.A. Cox looked at Malachi as he winked at him. Malachi's attorney leaned over to him to tell him something quietly.

"Don't worry about nothing he is saying, he has no facts, no statements at all." Malachi nodded when he said that. He leaned back in his seat and took a sip of water.

D.A. Cox looked at the judge.

"That will be all, Your Honor, thank you."

"You may be seated, Mr. Cox. You may take the floor, Mr. Anderson."

"Thank you, Your Honor." Attorney Anderson stood up, fixed his tie and walked around the table.

"First, let me say that was some kind of picture that D.A. Cox painted for y'all of the court. But the one question I have to ask is, where are the facts to his statements? Let me put it to you this way. Michael Lawson did an outstanding job designing this courtroom. There is one fact to that statement we know is true. This courtroom has an outstanding design to it that is a true fact, but the question in the air is, did Michael Lawson design it? I myself don't know that answer, so I can't stand in this courtroom and say that's a fact, because it's not.

"Let's go over some facts that D.A. Cox made that are true. There have been multiple bodies pulled out of the East River, that is a true statement and also a fact. There are drugs flooding the streets of New York, another true statement and a fact. But what is not a true statement or a fact, is that he doesn't know if Malachi Williams is behind any of it. Just like I don't know if Michael Lawson designed this courtroom.

"That's the difference between a fact, and a statement. D.A. Cox did not prove to anyone in this courtroom that Malachi Williams is behind any of this. He just made a statement that he was, but where are the facts behind his statement? I will let y'all, the people of the court, think about that for a second. That's all I have to say, Your Honor."

"Then you may be seated, Mr. Anderson." After two more hours of debates, the judge hit his gavel.

"Court is adjourned till tomorrow at 9:00 am. That will be all." Malachi looked at his attorney as he was getting up.

"Like I told you before, we have this trial in the bag. It's a win-win for us, trust me."

"The judge said tomorrow the witness will take the stand."

"Yeah, tomorrow you will look at Jaheem face-to-face as he tells your story in black and white." Malachi nodded. "But don't worry about that. I have a plan for that already."

"Me too, I'll see you tomorrow morning, Mr. Anderson." Malachi patted his attorney on the shoulders and walked off to where Kareem and Jazmine were waiting on him by the limo. He shook Kareem's hand and kissed Jazmine on the cheek as they got into the limo.

"Tomorrow, Jaheem is coming to court to take the stand against me." Jazmine looked at Malachi when he said that.

"We know, we heard everything on the radio," Kareem said.

"I'ma need both of y'all to do something. It's a rule I said we would never break. But in this case, we will have to bend it."

"I don't care if we have to break that bitch, Malachi, what's up?" Malachi lowered his head and lit his cigar and smiled at Kareem and Jazmine.

"This is what I need y'all to do tonight." Both of them leaned in as Malachi talked.

**

"Larry, we have a problem."

"And what is that?"

"It's been talks amongst the families about you and Malachi."

"And who is starting this confusion and bullshit amongst the families?"

"From what I was told, it's Peter and Robert, they had a secret meeting between the two of them." Larry looked at David as he smoked his cigar. He got up from behind his desk, walked to his office window and looked at the rain, as it fell from the sky and made puddles of water into the dirt. "I think it's time we have our own secret meeting with Peter if you get what I'm saying, David."

"I know what you are saying and honestly, I think it's about time. You would think he wouldn't want to poke the bear no more, but some people just don't get it until the bear turns on them, and all they have left is a spirit looking at a lifeless body. I'll set the meeting up for this week." Larry looked at David and nodded as he turned around and looked back out the window.

Chapter 25

Malachi stepped out of the limo, he looked at the two local news teams outside the courthouse recording live. He waved to everyone as he walked inside the courtroom, where his attorney was waiting on him. The courtroom was packed with family members of the victims, two news teams, and the jury. Malachi took his seat at the table next to his attorney.

"Today, you get to look into the eyes of Jaheem Smith, the district attorney's star witness against you. Are you ready for this?"

"Yeah, let's get it over with. I have my own star witness coming to the courtroom today." Attorney Anderson looked at Malachi funny when he said that. At that time the judge walked into the courtroom.

"All rise for The Honorable Judge Millz." Everyone stood up. The judge took his seat.

"You may all be seated." Everyone took their seats. "Mr. Cox, you may call your first witness." D.A. Cox stood up.

"I would like to call Malachi Williams to the stand." Malachi stood up and fixed his tie and walked to the stand and took his seat. After the bailiff swore him in, he looked up at the District Attorney.

"May you please state your name for the court?"

"Malachi Larmarr Williams."

"Malachi, is it true that you are the head of your own crime family?" D.A. Cox asked him.

"If you are asking me am I the head of my own household, yes I am, Mr. Cox. But a crime family? No, I am not." Malachi looked D.A. Cox dead in the eyes.

"So, you are saying right here and now today in court that you are not the head of any crime family?"

"I'm saying right here right now in this courtroom to be the head of a crime family there must be some crimes that were committed, Mr. Cox." D.A. Cox took a deep breath and pointed his finger at Malachi.

"There were crimes committed. Murders, kidnappings, extortion and aggravated assaults that all have your name attached to them, saying you are the ringleader to this organized crime group."

"And you heard stories that Peter Pan can fly, and a cow can jump over the moon, that don't mean it's true. D.A. Cox, a man in your position should know that."

"Mr. Williams, let's not get off track, have you ordered hits on over twenty people in New York City, including mob bosses?" Malachi leaned forward and looked D.A. Cox dead in the eyes.

"No, D.A. Cox, I have not."

"You know what, Mr. Williams, I'm not going to keep going in circles with you. The truth will come out today. Your Honor, I have no more questions for the witness."

"You may be seated, Mr. Cox. Mr. Anderson, your witness." Attorney Anderson stood up.

"I have no questions, Your Honor."

"Ok then, Mr. Williams, you may take your seat back at your attorney's side." Malachi sat back down next to his attorney.

"Mr. Cox, do you have any more witnesses you wish to call?"

"Yes, Your Honor, I do. At this time, I would like to call Seth Pittman to the stand." D.A. Cox looked at Malachi and smiled. Malachi cut his eyes to the right as the door opened up and he and Jaheem looked at each other. Malachi never took his eyes off of him as he took his seat at the bench.

"Would you state your name for the court?"

"Seth Pittman." Jaheem looked at the courtroom doors as someone walked out.

"Your witness, Mr. Cox."

"Thank you, Your Honor. Mr Pittman, do you know the defendant, Malachi Williams?"

"Yes, I do."

"How do you know him?"

"I used to work for him."

"Can you point him out to the courtroom?"

"Yes, I can. He is the man sitting right next to the man with the gray suit on." Jaheem pointed right at Malachi. Malachi picked up a glass of water and took a sip.

"Mr. Pittman, has Malachi Williams ever ordered you to kill anybody?" Jaheem looked at Malachi, the courtroom was quiet, nobody said a word. Before Jaheem could say a word, the courtroom doors opened and Jaheem looked and saw Jazmine walking in the courtroom, holding his five-year-old daughter in her arms, as his baby mother walked in behind her and took a seat on the back row. Malachi looked back at them, then at Jaheem and winked his eye.

"Mr. Pittman, can you answer the question?" Jaheem shook his head.

"I'm sorry, what was the question again?" D.A. Cox took a deep breath.

"Has Malachi Williams ever asked you, or ordered you to kill anybody?"

When the D.A. asked Jaheem that question, he looked at Jazmine holding his child. She looked at him and ran her finger across his daughter's throat and winked at him. Jaheem looked back at Malachi. He knew the rules he'd broken, and he knew it was his life or his child's life now at hand, and he had to make a choice right then and there. A tear ran down his face as he looked at his daughter.

"No, everyone I killed, I did of my own free will. The bodies in the East River, I did on my own. The drive-by shootings I did on my own, and the car bombings I did on my own. I have killed more people in New York City than John Gotti and Sammy the Bull. Everything I did was because I envied Malachi Williams. I was trying to set him up to make him take the fall for everything, that's how I knew where all the bodies were. I did everything of my own free will without Malachi's knowledge."

D.A. Cox couldn't believe what he was hearing. The court was in an uproar. Detectives Oldham and Benlose looked at D.A. Cox. The news team was taking pictures, the judge was banging his gavel and Malachi's attorney looked at him like he couldn't believe what he just heard.

"Mr. Pittman, you are under oath."

"I know this, Mr. Cox, and I just admitted the truth on live TV and in this courtroom. I killed them people of my own free will, D.A. Cox." D.A. Cox looked at Jaheem with the hate in his eyes that would put the fear of death in the devil's heart.

"I have no more questions, Your Honor, for the witness."

"Then you may be seated. Your witness, Attorney Anderson"

Mr. Anderson got up and walked up to Jaheem.

"Mr. Pittman, I have one question for you. Has Malachi Williams ever asked you to do anything against the law?"

"No, not once, never."

"I'm done, Your Honor."

"Then you may be seated. That is all for the day, court will continue tomorrow at 9:00 am." Malachi looked at his attorney.

"Like I said, I had my own star witness coming to court today. I'll see you tomorrow." Malachi looked in the faces of D.A. Cox, Detectives Benlose and Oldham as he walked out of the courtroom. He looked at all the people and threw two thumbs up. One of the reporters stopped him.

"Mr. Williams, how do you feel after that testimony today by Mr. Pittman?"

"I'm grateful for his honesty today." He waved to the camera and walked off to his limo.

Chapter 26

Can someone please tell me what the fuck happened in the court-room today?" D.A. Cox said as he looked at Detectives Benlose and Oldham.

"I don't fucking know. I'm still searching for answers."

"And I found the answers both of y'all are looking for, Mr. Cox and Oldham. He had no choice." Detective Oldham and D.A. Cox looked at Detective Benlose when he said that.

"What you mean, he ain't have no choice?"

"Just what I said, D.A. Cox. Let me show you something that *Eyewitness Five News* team caught on camera." Detective Benlose played the news recording back to the day of the trial, where Jazmine walked in the courtroom holding Jaheem daughter. He paused the tape on her holding Jaheem's daughter.

"You see, he had no choice. It was Malachi's life in prison, or his daughter dead in a grave, so what he did was give up his life to save his daughter's." D.A. Cox and Detective Oldham couldn't believe what they were seeing.

"He threatened his child's life in front of all of us. We were too blind to see it, because we were so focused on Malachi. Fuck me!"

"You are a hundred percent right, Mr. Cox. The question is where do we go from here?"

"There is only one thing we can do if we want to get Malachi. We have to drop all charges against him and start a secret indictment against him. That's the only way we can get him, Detective. We can still use the evidence we have on him to help with the case." Both detectives nodded as they looked at the screen as Jazmine was holding his daughter.

"Let's get this motherfucker," Detective Benlose said.

***

"Malachi, what is the attorney saying about the trial now?"

"It's already in the bag, Kareem. Thumbs up, John Gotti."

"That's what the fuck I'm talking about. Now, what are we going to do about Jaheem's ass?" Malachi lit his cigar and walked to the window and looked out of it.

"Jaheem knows the rules, we don't have to worry about him no more. The next conversation that comes up with Jaheem's name will be talking about his death."

"Are you sure of that? We don't even know where they are keeping him at." Malachi pulled his cigar.

"We don't need to know where they are keeping him at, he knows what he has to do already."

"Say no more then."

"Call a meeting for the family, we all need to talk."

"I'll do that now." Malachi watched as Kareem walked out his office to do what he was told to do.

Chapter 27

"We've known each other for over fifteen years, Peter. I looked at you as a friend, that rare someone I can trust in the mob. But I saw something was different in you that nobody else saw, and now I question myself after all these years." Peter looked around the old run-down farmyard, then back at Larry.

"I never gave you a reason why you shouldn't trust me. I have always been loyal and up front with you. So, I ask myself, where is all of this coming from?" Larry pulled on his cigar before talking.

"Peter... trust, loyalty and respect. You should know if you fuck up one, you lose all three. I know about the secret meetings with the other families you've been having behind my back." Peter looked at Larry in a state of shock.

"Don't look like that, Peter, what happens in the dark always comes to the light."

"You think I betrayed you? When you was the one who put a nigga before the mob? Where was your loyalty to us? Your race? Then you had him kill Grunt, Washington, and Lee... like you said, everything that happens in the dark always comes to the light. So, don't stand here telling me I'm wrong for putting the mob first. That's where my loyalty is at, Larry." Larry nodded and smiled at Peter.

"You are a hundred percent right. I put a nigga before the mob, because that nigga knows what real loyalty is, Peter."

"And I guess we don't, Larry?" Peter was looking at Larry when David grabbed him from behind, put a needle into his neck and pressed down on it, causing Peter to go to sleep. They picked Peter up and placed him in the car. Larry watched as David put a .38 revolver in Peter's hand and pointed the gun under his chin. He made sure his head was leaned back against the headrest, then he pulled the trigger one time, blowing the top part of his head on the ceiling of the car. He then let his arm drop down on his lap, closed the car door and looked at Larry.

"What now?"

"We go home and wait to hear the news that Peter Drews' body was found in the car, dead by suicide, David." David nodded as they both walked to the limo and got in and drove off.

***

Jaheem sat in the chair in his cell, reading over the letter he wrote to his daughter, Promise.

Beautiful black queen to be, I love you more than you will ever know. This letter is the last time you will hear from me. My days are over. I made a lot of bad choices in life and because of my choices, I have to choose my life or yours. So, as I write this letter, just know I will love you forever and a day. Death is not the end. This letter is sealed with a kiss, and I chose my life to save yours. Please forgive me, ladybug, forever and a day. My heart to yours.

Love, Daddy.

Jaheem's eyes spilled teardrops on the letter. He kissed the paper and placed it on the table in his cell. He refused to ask God for forgiveness, because of the things he did, he already knew there was a spot in hell waiting for him. He was just waiting to get to his bed and look the devil in his face. Jaheem took the sheet and climbed to the top of his cell and tied it on the bars. Then he wrapped it around his neck and closed his eyes as he jumped off the bars, hanging himself.

Chapter 28

Robert sat in his living room watching the news, when there was breaking news and they showed pictures of Peter Drews' car at the old farm.

The news reporter's voice droned, "As you look at the car behind me, for y'all who don't know, that is mob boss Peter Drews' car. Local authorities found Peter Drews' dead body inside the car, from what we've been told he committed suicide. Peter Drews was known for the fear he put in the heart of New York City as a crime boss over the Gambino family. Hold on one second, we have more breaking news.

"I am being told Seth Pittman, who testified against Malachi Williams in the murder trial yesterday, has also committed suicide by hanging himself in his cell. The cell block officers found him this morning as they were feeding breakfast trays. There was no chance of recovery for him. He was pronounced dead on the scene. Stay tuned for more updates on both men, found dead by suicide."

Robert couldn't believe what he just seen on the news before he could reach for his phone. It started to ring, he picked it up and heard Walter's voice on the other end.

"Robert, I knew Peter for fifteen years. He wasn't the type to kill himself, not at all. Something ain't right with this story."

"I already know. I just seen the news Peter was murdered. I'm not going for the bullshit that he killed himself, not at all. Keep your family under control, let me make some calls and I'll call you in a few days, when I've made sense of this."

"I'll be waiting to hear from you." Robert hung up the phone and finished watching the news.

***

"You have to be fucking kidding me. Fuck! Fuck! Fuck! This can't be happening like this." District Attorney Cox paced his office floor as he watched the news. His face was bloodshot red. He was so upset. He sat down behind his desk and had to face the fact that Malachi Williams was now, the untouchable. Nothing more would give him more pleasure than to see Malachi die by lethal injection. Just to watch him take his last breath. Malachi was a killer and he hated everything about him. He promised himself before this was over, Malachi would be in a prison jumpsuit with the stamp that said, *State Property*.

Chapter 29

"Stupid is knowing the truth, but still believing the lie," Malachi said as he looked at everyone at the table. He picked the newspaper up and threw it in the middle of the table. Everyone looked at the front-page headline, it read, *Crime boss Peter Drews dead by suicide*. On the other half of the paper it said, *Seth Pittman dead by suicide*. The bottom half of the newspaper said, *Malachi Williams, the untouchable crime boss, the new king of New York*.

"The mob knows what it is now. A nigga runs New York City and there ain't shit they can do about it. How the fuck are they going to stop us? That motherfucker on the front page of that paper was a dishonorable son of a bitch. He was a traitor and a deceiver. He betrayed our trust. He was a snitch, a rat, he turned on us to save his own cowardly ass. Jaheem was a fucking rat, period, but you know what? Still, we stand.

"You know why? Because we stand on honor, trust and loyalty. If my heart was really cold, I woulda sent his fucking daughter's heart to him in prison in a box. But you know what, we are going to pop the bottle. Everybody, from street hustlers to the mob, and even crooked cops are going to pay, and if they don't pay, rock a bye they ass." Malachi looked at everyone at the table then lit his cigar. Malachi blew the smoke out of his mouth before speaking.

"Shoot or get shot, everyone is on the grocery list. I don't give a fuck how they are eating on the block. If a pimp selling pussy, he owe us, point blank. You get it? Meeting over. There ain't shit else to say."

***

"Walter, you are the captain of this ship now, and what you need to be worried about is who killed Peter. We need to know everyone who had they hand in his murder. Peter ain't kill himself at all."

"I know he ain't Robert. I'm thinking Malachi," Walter and Robert sat on the bench looking at the sun's reflection off of the lake as it was setting, with their bodyguards behind them.

"Walter, it wasn't Malachi, Peter would have never gone to meet him by himself. If anything, he would have sent Malachi up to be killed. I hate to say it but, in my eyes, Larry played a part in Peter's death, if he wasn't the one who killed him."

"Robert, if I find out that Larry had anything to do with Peter's murder, I will skin him alive before I cut his fucking throat." Walter looked at Robert with anger in his eyes.

"We will find out soon. And remember what you just said."

"I won't forget it."

"Good because if he did. What you just said, honor that." Robert got up and nodded at his bodyguard as they walked off, leaving Walter and his men at the park.

Chapter 30

Walter sat in the warehouse, with two of his men standing on each side of him. He looked at his watch as the warehouse doors opened up and two officers dragged Casper into the warehouse, beaten badly and bleeding. Both of Walter's men walked up to the officers and grabbed Casper out of their hands. The officers nodded at Walter and walked out of the warehouse. Walter watched as his men tied Casper down to the chair. Walter took a rag out of his back pocket and patted his forehead with it as he looked at Casper.

"Me and you both know that you are not going to come out of this alive, so I'm not going to give you no false hope that you are. But I will give you a choice on how you die, you can die with a lot of pain or with a single bullet, that will be your choice." Casper looked up at Walter with blurry vision, then at both of the men he had with him, then back at Walter then he spit in his face.

"Cracker, my whole life been nothing but pain, so let my last moments follow the same path." Walter was wiping the spit out his face as Casper was talking. He looked at Casper with hate in his eyes.

"Beat him and don't stop till something breaks." Casper looked at one of Walter's men as he put brass knuckles on his hand, he smiled and looked at Casper.

"You put them on, now let's see if you hit like a bitch, motherfucker." Casper got punched so hard in the face, the blow broke his nose and knocked him out at the same time. As he flipped backwards in the chair to the floor, they beat Casper with a bat and crowbar until his arm and leg was broken. The pain woke him up and knocked him out two times. Casper was on the floor, still tied to the chair and bleeding from the mouth.

"I can do this all day. Now, I want to know, did Malachi have anything to do with Peter's murder?"

"You doing all this for a fucking cracker, who killed himself? I thought this was about you finding out I was fucking your daughter," Casper said with short breaths as he was coughing up blood with tears in his eyes. Walter walked up to him and kicked him in the face two times.

"Peter might have killed himself, but I will promise you one thing, tonight I'ma be the one who kills you." Walter stuck out his hand at one of his men. "Pistol," he said without taking his eyes off Casper. Walter took the gun from his guard and looked down at Casper.

"After I kill you, I'ma hang your body off the bridge. Then I'm do the same thing to Malachi."

"Malachi is going to slice your throat and watch you bleed. I might not be here to see it, but I promise you, you are going to die by his hands." Walter sucked his teeth and nodded.

"Hey, I guess we will see, won't we?" Walter shot Casper two times in the head, point blank range, killing him.

"Hang his body over the Brooklyn Bridge and meet me back at the pool hall." Walter walked out of the warehouse, leaving his men behind, and Casper in a pool of blood.

***

Malachi stood next to the window in his office smoking a cigar when Kareem walked in his office. "Malachi." Malachi turned around, looked at Kareem and pulled his cigar.

"I don't want to talk about it. Find out who did it, and have them and whoever they are with, bodied. Casper ain't going to die alone." Malachi turned back around and looked back out the window. All he heard was his office door closing as Kareem walked out.

Chapter 31

"Jazmine, Malachi wants blood over Casper, and he don't care whose blood it is. He wants answers and a body count." Jazmine looked around as she drove through Brooklyn, trying to find out who killed Casper.

"Bishop, this don't make no sense. Motherfuckers know how we get down, why would they play with fire? Knowing they are going to get burned."

"Some motherfuckers just have a death wish and can't wait to die."

"You got to be fucking kidding me. Look, Bishop, this motherfucker lost his damn mind." Bishop looked to the right and saw someone driving Casper's car.

"What the fuck? I just told you niggas got a death wish, Jazmine." Bishop pulled his gun out and put his hoodie on.

"Yo, follow that nigga, let's see what he knows before we body his ass."

"What the fuck you thought, I was going to let him drive off? Bishop, how the fuck you sound?" Jazmine and Bishop followed Casper's car as the driver was blasting Birdman and Lil Wayne's, "Stuntin Like My Daddy." They followed him to 114th Street and as he was getting out of the car, Jazmine pulled up next to him and popped the trunk. Bishop jumped out the car and smacked him in the face with the gun, knocking him out. He grabbed him before he hit the ground and threw him in the trunk, jumped in Casper's car and drove off, with Jazmine right behind him.

***

Detective Oldham walked up on Calvin Reeves. Calvin looked at him, as Detective Oldham pulled his badge out and showed it to Calvin.

"So, you have a badge and a gun, I take it you are a cop. Now that you showed me your badge, what do you want, cop?"

"I just want to have a word with you, that's all. We are on two different sides of the law, but we do have one thing in common." Calvin looked at Detective Oldham and smiled.

"How do you think we have something in common?" Detective Benlose smiled as he lowered his head and lit a Newport.

"One name is all I have to say."

"And what's the name, Detective?"

"Malachi." Calvin looked at Detective Oldham with hate in his eyes.

"Yeah, I'm still trying to put it together on how a nigga became bigger than the mob. Ain't it funny how two people that was going against Malachi, ended up dead by suicide on the same day, within hours of each other? This is how I see things, Calvin. You can help me put this son of a bitch away, or you can watch a nigga take over your city. Or maybe one day I can open up the newspaper and read the headline that might say, Calvin Reeves, mob boss dead by suicide. "See, there is one thing I know about the mob. That most motherfuckers in the mob are the ones you don't hear about."

Calvin looked at Detective Oldham because he knew he was right. Detective Oldham placed his card on Calvin's car window and walked off. Calvin picked up the card and looked around before getting in his car and driving off.

Chapter 32

Malachi walked into the warehouse and looked at the man tied to the chair. He pulled his cigar and looked at Bishop and Jazmine.

"Is he talking yet?" Jazmine walked up to Malachi.

"Yeah, he said he saw a cop pull over Casper and locked him up and drove off. He waited a few minutes and took his car."

"Did he say was the cop white, black, blue…yellow, green…how the fuck the cop look?" Jason looked at Malachi with a busted-up eye and lip.

"It was Griffin who pulled him over and locked him up." Malachi pulled his cigar before talking.

"Kill him and bring me Griffin."

Malachi walked off and Jason screamed, "No! No, man, don't kill me! I ain't have shit to do with it!" Jazmine walked up to Jason and put the gun to his head and pulled the trigger. The gunshot echoed through the warehouse.

"Get me Griffin, Casper will not die alone."

***

"Just look at him chopped up, you have a leg over there, and an arm over there. Detective Benlose, the mob is going to want blood for this." Detective Benlose looked around at the crime scene, took a deep breath and covered his mouth before talking.

"So, you think this is a war that just got started, Oldham?"

"Look around, Benlose, sometimes their behavior is your answer. Come on, we need to get a head start on this before it gets out of control." Detective Benlose looked around one more time before walking off.

***

"Stacy, look at you. We just let you out of jail not even seventy-two hours ago and you are already back on the block selling yourself." Officer Griffin looked at Stacy as she was leaning against the wall of the store, high off drugs.

"What do I need to get a pass, Griffin? What, you want your dick sucked again?" Officer Griffin smiled and pointed to his car, Stacy shook her head and walked to the police car. As he opened up the back door to let her inside the car, he looked around before getting in the car and driving off. Kareem and Jazmine looked at Officer Griffin from their car down the block.

"You would think a dirty cop like Griffin would move a lot better, Jazmine, come on let's see where he's taking her."

"I know where he is taking her already, Kareem. The look in his eyes the way he's moving. He is taking her somewhere so he can get some pussy."

"Sure, you are right, let's go."

***

Walter sat behind the desk, talking on the phone when Robert Pacino walked in the office, and took a seat in front of his desk.

"Let me call you back, Lil John, Robert just walked in." Walter hung up the phone and looked at Robert as he lit his cigar.

"This is new, you coming by. What can I do for you, Robert?"

"Walter, great men are not born great, they grow great, and I hate to say it but that is our friend Malachi. And if we don't kill him soon, I have a feeling you might be next, waiting for your body to be found by someone."

"So, how the fuck do you want to kill this nigga?"

"The fuck if I know. The first thing we need to do is find out where he is staying and who is working for him. We need to know who is backing him up now."

"Yeah, that shouldn't be hard, we just have to look for a black man talking to a white man in a nice suit."

"Yeah, let me say this before I leave you, Walter. Do the work others aren't willing to do and you'll get the things others will never have. That was Peter's problem, he never wanted to do the work that needed to get done."

Robert got up and walked out the office, not saying another word to Walter.

***

"You always got me sucking your dick, but never give me no money. This blackmail is going to stop, Griffin, you can take me back to jail for all of this I have to do."

"Just be quick and quiet and keep sucking my dick till I tell you when to stop, before I do take you to jail with mo dope charges." Stacy rolled her eyes and did what she was told.

"Just look at him, Jazmine, in the car thinking no one can see him by the old pound. Come on, let's deliver the message Malachi wants."

Chapter 33

Captain Fuller was watching the news, when his phone went off. He put the TV on mute and answered the phone.

"Captain Fuller speaking."

"Captain, this is Detective Benlose, I'm down here by the old pound. We have an officer down, you need to see this."

"You have to be fucking kidding me, who is it?"

"Officer Griffin."

"I'm on my way." Detective Benlose walked back to where Detective Oldham was at.

"The captain is on his way now. I have never seen no shit like this before, Oldham." Detective Benlose couldn't stop looking at Officer Griffin as he laid in a pool of blood with his eyes open and his tongue pulled through his neck.

"You remember you asked me if a war was about to start?

"Yeah."

"This is the second body we found this way. The war already started, Benlose, it's already started." Detective Benlose looked as the captain's car pulled up and he stepped out.

***

"If you two are here, that means my message was delivered, right?" Kareem handed Malachi his phone. Malachi looked at the pictures Kareem took of Officer Griffin, then handed back the phone to Kareem.

"You know what they say, when you die with your eyes open, it was meant to be. I knew I could count on you two, now the ball is in their court."

SAYNOMORE

Chapter 34

Walter was reading the newspaper about Officer Griffin's murder, that's when he heard a knock at the door. He laid the paper down on his desk.

"Come in." Green opened the door and walked into his office. Walter picked up the paper and showed him what the headlines said.

"You see what this says? Officer murdered, tongue pulled through his neck." Walter shook his head as he slammed the paper back down on his desk.

"You know what, Green? I want to hurt this nigga so bad that he will never come back at me. Griffin was on my fucking payroll. You know how fucking hard it is to get a good cop to work for you under the table? You know, working for the mob, you put your life, freedom and family behind you, the mob in front of you and Griffin knew that. Now he's fucking dead with his tongue pulled through his neck. I want blood for this." Green looked at the newspaper on Walter's desk and nodded.

"What do you want done?" Walter leaned back in his chair, placed his hand on his chin and looked off from him, out the window.

"The nigger is smart... I'll give him that. Don't nobody know where he's at. My judge was supposed to bury him, he beat the case, then became a ghost. We need to flush the nigga out. Start having his shops and stores shot up, make him come after us." Walter tapped his hand twice on his desk after saying that. Green knocked two times on his desk and got up and walked out the office.

***

D.A. Cox walked into Captain Fuller's office, where Detectives Oldham and Benlose were waiting for him. He took a seat next to both detectives.

"I'm sorry I'm late, but I had a very busy morning, and my boss is on top of my head. We need to face the fact that Malachi Williams is now the boss of bosses. He's the boss of the boss of the boss. We had him and we let him go. We need to work on getting

117

him back. Now I know we already had this conversation, but now we need to show action behind it, we need Malachi Williams behind bars looking at life. We need him off our streets, we need to take back control of our streets and we can't do that with Malachi Williams still out there." D.A. Cox looked at everyone in the room after talking.

"D.A. Cox, we understand what you are saying but this is not the Wild Wild West, this is New York City. We can't go around breaking the law. We all want to see Malachi Williams taken down, but let's also face the facts, Malachi Williams is the untouchable don. We don't even see him anymore. He points a finger, says a word, and makes a phone call. Bam, a motherfucker is dead. When we had the chance to take him down, nobody wanted to give us the green light. Now the D.A.'s office wants us to go up against NYC and guess what? Newsflash! Malachi Williams has Brooklyn in his back pocket, D.A. Cox." Detective Oldham looked D.A. Cox dead in the eyes after saying that.

"Detective, let me have a word with D.A. Cox alone." Detective Oldham looked at Detective Benlose and got up as both of them walked out the office closing the door behind them.

"D.A. Cox, what's all we need to get something to stick on Malachi?"

"We need him on videotape we need him dead to the wrong, that's the only way, Captain."

"Come see us in a few weeks." D.A. Cox nodded and shook Captain Fuller's hand before walking out his office.

Chapter 35

"Malachi, you know what I like about you?"

"No, tell me, Larry." Larry took a sip of his drink before talking.

"You listen, but this is what I want you to do, pay attention to the little shit. Ain't no problem too small not to go unnoticed. Casper was the messenger, but you are the fucking message they kill you they deliver it. The small problems are the ones unnoticed. Cops fucking informers, you get it."

"Yeah, I do, that's why I became a ghost to stay out the eyesight of the people, Larry."

"You think a ghost can't be seen? If so, you are wrong. There are three things you need to know, because if you break one, you lose all three."

"And what is that?"

Trust, respect, and loyalty. When you don't keep your word, Malachi, you lose credibility."

"I understand."

"Good, now I asked you for one favor."

"And what's that?"

"When you kill Walter... before you take his life, let him know Larry said it wasn't personal with Peter, it was just strictly business."

"I will," Malachi got up and shook Larry's hand before leaving. He had Kareem waiting for him in the car.

"How did everything go, Malachi?" Malachi pulled out a cigar and lit it before talking.

"Good, like always just business talk." Kareem nodded his head and didn't say nothing else. Malachi's limo pulled up in the front of Admiral's Row Apartments, he looked at Kareem before stepping out the car.

"We need to find Walter and kill him." Kareem nodded.

"I'll get on that right away." Malachi opened the limo door and stepped out. He looked to the left where the playground was and saw a kid out there holding something in his hand. As a crackhead walked out the playground, Malachi looked at Kareem and walked to where the kid was. Malachi walked up to him and looked down at him.

"What's up, little man?" The kid looked up at Malachi and Kareem and took a step back.

"What's up?"

"You tell me what you got in your hand right there?"

"Nothing," Malachi smiled and looked at Kareem when he said that."

"Let me ask you this, do you know who I am?" The kid nodded. "Yeah, Malachi."

"So, if you know who I am, then you should know not to lie to me. So, what you got in your hands, little man?" The kid opened his hand and showed Malachi the bagged-up crack.

"How old are you?"

"Ten."

"What's your name, little man?"

"Tilmen." Malachi sat on the bench in the park.

"Tilmen, come sit next to me." Tilmen sat next to Malachi.

"You know the dope game ends one or two ways, and if you are good at what you do, three. Do you know how it could end for you?"

"Jail if I get caught."

"Yeah, that's one way, but you could also be killed and get somebody in your family hurt."

"I know, but my mom need the money. She cries a lot so I have to help her."

"Your mother gave you those drugs?"

"No."

"So, where you get them from?"

"I stole them from a guy she was with." Malachi looked at Kareem.

"Come on, little man, take me to your mother." Tilmen got off the bench and walked with Malachi and Kareem to his mother's apartment door. They heard yells and things breaking from outside the door. Malachi opened the door and looked at Tilmen's mother on the floor crying, and a man standing over her with a gun in his hand. He looked at Malachi and moved away from her. Malachi looked at Kareem as he walked up to the dude and took the gun out of his hand.

"What type of man puts his hands on a female?"

"She stole from me."

"No, she didn't, I got your shit. So, you are trapping in my apartments, nigga, behind my back… that's like a spit in my fucking face." The dude looked at Kareem, then back at Malachi.

"It was just a few plays, man, that's all."

"You know I really don't give a fuck if it was one or ten, you still fucking did it. Sit in the fucking chair, nigga, and put your hand on the fucking arm rest. Now, motherfucker, I ain't playing." Everyone watched as he sat in the chair and put his hand on the arm rest.

"You are going to learn a lesson today and get a pass at the same time. You lucky I don't take your fucking life, nigga." Malachi pulled his gun out and shot him in the hand. The dude jumped up, holding his hand screaming.

"Nigga, stop that crying shit, niggas get shot every day. Now, here are the rules. If I ever see you around here again, niggas will never find your body. And if you go to the police, I'll skin you alive before you fucking die. Now, get the fuck up out of here." Kareem opened the door for him to walk out. Malachi looked at Tilmen's mother still on the floor, holding Tilmen in her arms. Malachi took a seat at the table and looked at Tilmen.

"Tilmen, come here." Tilmen looked at his mother then went to Malachi. "Come have a seat next to me." Tilmen sat next to Malachi. Malachi looked at him.

"Remember the talk we just had in the park, where I told you the drug game can get you killed or someone hurt? Yeah, look at what just happened to your mother. She coulda got hurt if we ain't come up here in time, you see that, right?"

"Yeah, I do. I was just trying to help her."

"I know, little man. Trust me, I do."

"Is he gone to come back?"

"Not if he don't want to die. Now, give me the rest of everything you had." Tilmen's mother looked at him as he handed Malachi the baggies of dope. Malachi put them in his pocket, pulled out a knot of hundreds and counted out two thousand, and handed it to Tilmen. "Now, I don't want to catch you on the block again, ok?"

"Ok, Malachi. I won't no more, I promise."

"Good, now let me tell you about a promise and your word. When you don't keep your word, you lose credibility, and self-respect is always your first priority over any relation." Malachi got up and handed Tilmen's mother his card.

"If you ever need anything, call me. And I'll be around to come pick Tilmen up sometime this week." Malachi and Kareem walked out the apartment, closing the door behind them.

Chapter 36

"Jazmine, all the money is in the two bags over there on the floor in the corner." Jazmine walked over to the bags and looked inside.

"How much in each bag?"

"Five hundred thousand, it's a cool million together." Jazmine zipped the bags back up.

"Help me bring them to the car." Jazmine picked up one of the bags and walked out the apartment to her car.

"Bishop, we more lookouts on this block. We beat the NYPD and we was dead to the wrong in every way, so you know who is going to come at us now. The FBI and niggas don't beat them."

"Jazmine, I'm on that, I'll get a few more guys down here to look out."

"Good, because last time I got caught slipping, and I coulda got bodied by them rude boys."

"Jazmine, I'm on it. I got you, homie."

"Good, because I don't want to do another body count." Bishop put the bag in the trunk of the car. Jazmine kissed his cheek before getting in the car and driving off.

***

"Yoo, P-Lo, how we looking out here?"

"Great, my dude. We already sixty thousand for the day and it ain't even 3:00 pm yet, Kilo."

"Yeah, Malachi snapped when he opened up shop over here."

"Yeah, he ain't give no fucks. This was Peter's spot, when he said the takeover, he meant that shit."

"Fucking right he did."

"You see them two niggas over there, that used to be Peter's auto parts shop about two years ago. Now this fucking nigga think he could take over Peter turf, let's show them what time it is."

"Let's go, Mickey."

"P-Lo, look, who in that blue van over there?" P-Lo looked, but before he could say a word, shots were coming from the side. Kilo watched as P-Lo's body hit the ground. He pulled his gun out and got shot two times in the chest. His body hit the side of the wall before it hit the ground. Green waved to the blue van as he stood over Kilo and P-Lo's body. He moved to the side as the van crashed through the front of the store, all everyone heard was gunshots and people yelling.

Then the van backed out of the store and drove off. Within minutes, the store was in flames. Green looked around before leaving two dead bodies outside the store, and five dead bodies inside. This was a message from Walter to Malachi in black and white, letting him know who owned Brooklyn.

Chapter 37

"Malachi, we was hit last night, not only did they kill five of our guys, but they burned the store down with the work inside. And that's not it, our truck got hit with two hundred kilos, they got it." Malachi sat on the edge of the desk smoking a cigar, listening to Kareem as he talked. He couldn't believe what he was hearing. He got up off the desk and walked to the window and looked out of it.

"Does anybody know where Walter is at?"

"Maybe the fish market downtown, if I would have to guess." Malachi nodded.

"Walter's not slow, he not like Peter, he's going to be waiting on us to hit back. I always knew he would hit that spot. The shipment, let them have it. Walter is a little dog trying to take a big dog's food. He just demonstrated that by stealing our supply. If the shoe was on the other foot, I would have burned it. Have someone watch the fish market. We ain't going after a pawn. Walter wants to be the king. We are going to kill him and take his crown." Malachi turned around and looked at Kareem, nodded and walked out the office.

***

"Walter, Malachi just got that message. We burned the store down, killed his guys and got one of his shipments that was pulling up. So, we got two wins back-to-back." Walter took a sip of his gin and smiled.

"Every dog got his day, and a mad dog gets put to sleep. This nigga going to strike back. He might be sitting back right now thinking on how to do it. I want eyes everywhere. If you see a nigga where he don't supposed to be on my block, bury they ass. We ain't taken no chances with these monkeys. Remember, this war ain't about who's right, it's about who's left and Peter ain't understand that. That's why he's dead, six feet in a pine box and still I stand."

"I'll put a few more guys at every spot, boss." Walter nodded.

"Green?"

"Yeah, boss?"

"You always get the job done, that's why I put my trust in you."

"Thanks, boss."

Chapter 38

Bishop sat in the black BMW and watched the fish market as Green walked out of it. Talking to two people, he pulled his gun out and cocked it back, and watched as they got into the car and drove off. In the back of his mind, he wanted to follow them, but he knew who he was there to get. So far, he counted eight men, plus the three that left, he'd watched the fish market for three hours.

He was about to leave when he saw a blue Town Car pull up and two detectives get out the car and wall inside. All eyes were on Detective Oldham and Detective Benlose as they walked into the fish market. They looked around before walking to the back door where there were two men guarding the door. They walked up to them and showed them their badges.

"Now, we can do this the nice way or the hard way. The nice way would be you two big guys can step to the side, so we can go talk with Walter, after one of you lets him know that there are two detectives out here. Or you can stand there like you don't know we are out here, or we are some nobodies and we can do it the hard way and turn this bitch upside down and put cases on all you mother-fuckers. And what you think Walter would have to say then after he gets out on bail? Attorneys and DA up his ass, now be a good boy and get your fucking master." Detective Oldham looked as one of the guards opened the door and stepped inside after Detective Benlose said what he said to them.

"Boss, you have two nigger detectives out here trying to talk to you. I would have ran them off, but they started talking about a shakedown and putting cases on us." Walter placed his cigar into an ashtray and picked up his bottle of water and took a sip.

"Go get them and let them in, let's hear what the NYPD have to say to me." When the doors opened up, both detectives walked inside and looked at Walter as he was lighting his cigar back up. He looked at both detectives before taking his seat behind his desk.

"Detectives, what can I do for you?"

"That's not the question that needs to be asked, Walter. The right question is, what can we do for you? Do you mind if we have a seat?"

"No, please sit down, can I get you something to drink?"

"No, thank you."

"So, tell me, what can I do for you two detectives?"

"I guess you ain't hear what I said when I first came in your office. Let me get to the point of why I'm here."

"Please do so,"

"This war you have going on with Malachi Williams needs to stop, and from the looks of it, you're losing."

"Is that what you think, Detective? I ain't know there was a war I was in." Walter pulled his cigar and leaned back in the chair looking at the detectives.

"When the NYPD is pulling white bodies out of the East River, dumpsters are burning, cars and all the blood drops and dead bodies come back to you. Do you want to see some of the pictures I have?"

"No. When you see one dead body, Detective, you have seen a hundred."

"Walter, you know what I like about the mob?"

"Detective, if you believe in the mob, then I guess you believe in the tooth fairy, the boogie man, and whatever other children's story you was told as a child."

"That's what I mean about the mob, it's just a children's story. But let me tell you what's not a children's story, the NYPD. And when we kick in your door and the D.A. puts them charges on you and everyone else, don't come to me trying to tell me a children's story that I already know the ending of, Walter."

"Detectives, I want to thank you for coming by to see me and trying to pick my brain. But if you don't mind, it's 2:00 pm and the New York Jets game is about to come on and I don't want to miss it. So, y'all can see your way out and have a blessed day." Detective Benlose smiled at Walter then looked at Detective Oldham as he got up.

"We will be seeing you around, Walter, enjoy your game." Detective Benlose dropped his card on Walter's desk before walking out of his office.

SAYNOMORE

Chapter 39

"Kareem, I sat outside that fish market all day and ain't see that motherfucker Walter, but I know he was in there, because them two detectives that have been popping up pulled up there today." Bishop took a sip of the soda he had in his hand as he looked at Kareem.

"So, you telling me they got heat on them too?"

"Yeah, them crackers are on fire, four hundred degrees."

"Say less, I'ma let Malachi know the police got their eyes on Walter." Kareem looked out the window and nodded.

"Kareem, I need to go see Jazmine."

"Go ahead, I'll call you in a little while."

"Cool, I'll be waiting." Bishop got up and walked out the office, leaving Kareem in his thoughts.

***

"So, you telling me Walter have the police breathing down his back too?"

"Yeah, that's what Bishop said, he told me they was there for a minute talking." Malachi pulled his cigar and smiled.

"You know what, Kareem, maybe it's time we make Detectives Oldham and Benlose' hearts pump Kool-Aid."

"What you have in mind?" Malachi licked his lips and gave Kareem an evil smile.

"Let's kidnap them." Kareem looked at Malachi as he pulled his cigar.

"Did I hear you right? Because you know we are talking about kidnapping detectives, right?"

"Yeah, you heard me right."

"So, are we going to rock-a-bye them?"

"No, just shake them up a little bit."

"Malachi, this shit is crazy, how the hell we going to kidnap cops?"

"With a crash and a boom."

"And we ain't going to kill them. We are going to let them walk away alive. I just want to make sure I'm hearing you right."

"You heard me right, now let's put this plan together, baby."

***

Detectives Benlose and Oldham sat in the front of the coffee shop, drinking a cup of coffee and talking, when the black SUV pulled up down the street.

"Kareem, are we really about to do this shit?"

"Yes, we are, Bishop. Trust me, I know what you are thinking already. Malachi lost his fucking mind, but Malachi is the boss, so let's get this done."

"So, how you want to do this?"

"When they get into the car and pull off, we are going to pull up in front of them. I'ma open the back door and shoot the front of the car up. I'ma grab the driver up and make the passenger get out. We are going to stick them with these needles put them to sleep and get the fuck on."

"Kareem, you said some shit that you might see in a movie, shit like this don't happen in real life."

"Well, today's the day we make a movie into real life." Bishop smiled and put his murder one on his face as they both watched Detectives Benlose and Oldham drink their coffee in front of the coffee shop.

"Now you and I both know Walter fed us some bullshit, and we have the D.A., chief, and captain breathing down our necks over some shit we tried to tell them about two years ago."

"Benlose, we are little fish in their sea, plus you already know how the cookie crumbles."

"Yeah, that's the fucked-up thing about it. We in the streets while they in the office."

"We are the do-boys, and they are the HFIC, now come on let's get up out of here" Benlose took a sip of his coffee.

"HFIC, Oldman?"

132

"Yeah, head fuckers in charge." Both of them started to laugh as they got up and walked off from the table.

"Let's pop the bottle, Bishop, it's time to rock and roll, they leaving now, homie. Bishop watched as they got into the car and started to drive off. Kareem looked at Bishop and nodded. As they drove past Detectives Benlose and Oldham, there were cars on both sides of them. Kareem walked to the back of the van with an M16 in his hands and was looking at Detective Benlose as he drove the car behind them.

"So, where are we headed first, Benlose?"

"I was thinking we will head down 114th Street. I have a CI down there that might give us a little bit of information on Malachi's crew."

"Let's see what we can find out then."

"Let's do it, Oldham, good cop, bad cop."

"Good cop, bad cop, Benlose." Benlose looked at the black van in front of them. When the van doors opened up, he stopped the car and looked in a state of shock as he saw the M16 pointed at them. Before he could say a word, bullets were flying at them. They both took cover, ducking down in the car. Kareem jumped out the van and with the back of the M16, he broke out the driver's side window and pointed the gun at them.

"Get out the fucking car. Move wrong, you fucking die, don't try me."

Detective Benlose looked at the M16 pointed at him. He closed his eyes as he got out of the car. Hands in the air, he took a deep breath and shook his head. Detective Oldham went to pull out his gun as Benlose was getting out of the car, when Bishop shot through the window, pointing the AR-15 at him. Oldham dropped his gun and stepped out of the car, hands in the air and walked around to the front of the car and got into the van with Benlose. People were recording everything with their phones. Kareem closed the van doors as Bishop drove off.

"Both of y'all motherfuckers on your stomachs now." As they laid on their stomachs, Kareem took their handcuffs and cuffed their hands behind their backs, then he put two paper bags over their heads and stuck them each with a needle, putting them to sleep within two minutes.

***

"Who the fuck kidnaps cops in broad daylight on Main Street?" Chief Ward and Captain Fuller looked around at the crime scene.

Captain Fuller walked to Detective Benlose's car and looked around it, when one of the officers walked up to him.

"Captain Fuller, you might want to take a look at this." Captain Fuller looked at Officer Malone as he held his cell phone out and showed him the video of both detectives getting kidnapped on *YouTube*, it already had sixty thousand views.

"You have to be fucking kidding me, let me see your phone, Officer. I have to show the chief this." Captain Fuller walked to Chief Ward and handed him the phone.

"Get the motherfucker who owns this van. I want to know who got my boys and I want they fucking head on a chopping block. I want every officer on the streets till we find out who did this, and we get our boys back." Captain Fuller took the phone back to the officer and did what Chief Ward said.

Chapter 40

Detective Benlose opened his eyes and looked around. His eyesight was blurry, and his head was pounding as if he got hit in the head with a jackhammer. His hands were tied up by chains to the ceiling. He looked to the right and saw Oldham in the same position, tied from the ceiling with the chains. He looked around again and saw he was in some type of garage. Nobody was around. His mouth was dry, he took a deep breath as he called Oldham's name.

"Oldham, Oldham, wake up. Wake up, buddy." Detective Oldham opened his eyes and shook his head as he was taken a short breath.

"Where are we, Benlose?"

"I don't know, the last thing I remember was getting a needle in my neck and passing out."

"How long you think we been here for?"

"I don't know, Oldham. There's no windows to look out of but we must've been here more than a few hours."

Both detectives looked when they heard the garage doors opening and saw a masked man walking, pushing a TV on a cart he stopped and looked at both of them. Then cut the TV on and turned around and walked out. The TV was playing the news, both of them started looking at the news.

"This is Rhonda Moore with *Fox 5 News*. Yesterday, right here on Main Street in Brooklyn, two detectives with the 34th Police Station were kidnapped at gunpoint. We do have everything on film. Now this video footage is disturbing."

Both detectives watched as they were set up from the start and how they were kidnapped. The news went off, then some words came across the TV screen, big and bold. *Your case is going to get you and your loved ones killed, know who you are dealing with, Detective Oldham, let this be the first and last warning.* Then pictures of his house and kids came on the screen, pictures of his kids at school and his wife picking them up. Then there was a picture of his kids, seen through the eye of an assault rifle.

Then the same thing happened with Detective Benlose, but not only his kids and wife, but his mother sitting on the porch of her house doing a word cross and drinking tea. Then the TV went blank. Both detectives looked at each other and in a state of shock, not believing what they'd just seen.

"Benlose, we coulda been dead… our family… what the fuck, man?" Detective Benlose was lost for words. That's when the doors opened up again. A man walked up to them and stuck them in the neck with the needle again, putting them to sleep.

Chapter 41

"Walter, there are police everywhere, it's hard to move out there. They are on the corner, walking into stores, they're running down the guys. There's no movement. Whoever kidnapped them detectives fucked a lot of shit up." Walter pulled on his cigar as Green was talking to him.

"This has Malachi's name all over it. Who else would kidnap cops?" Green shook his head, lost for words.

"This is what I want you to do, Green, keep all the guys off the streets we don't need no more heat on us, did anybody find out where this nigga is at?"

"Not yet, Walter. But I have a few guys already on it, boss."

"Good, keep me updated." Green nodded and turned around and walked out of Walter's office.

***

"This is crazy, every other block there is a damn roadblock. So now we have to take a thirty-minute detour because some cops have been kidnapped. Shaking my fucking head." Chad looked at Kim as they were going down the dark road next to the lake.

"Baby, you have to understand two gangsters kidnapped two detectives in broad daylight at gunpoint. It's all over the news and *YouTube*, this is big, baby." Chad nodded.

"I guess you are right, beautiful." Kim reached over and held Chad's hand as they rode down the dark road next to the lake. Kim looked out the window and saw two bodies lying next to the lake that looked like they were dead.

"Chad! Chad, stop the car! Stop! I think I just saw two dead bodies over there." Chad stopped the car and got out and walked over to the two bodies lying next to the lake. After a few seconds, he ran back to the car and pulled his phone out and dialed 911. Within fifteen minutes, twenty police officers were out there on the scene and Captain Fuller talking to Chad and Kim by the car.

SAYNOMORE

***

Larry sat in his living room watching the news as he drank his white wine, he knew Malachi was behind the kidnapping of the detectives. Malachi was playing chess at a new level, and it was only a matter of time before Walter would be laying in a pine box.

Chapter 42

"Malachi, it's time that this war with Walter gets put to an end."

"Are you for real, Larry, do you hear what you are saying?"

"Yeah, I do."

"This war will end when I kill Walter."

"Or if he kills you first. Malachi, you crossed the line when you kidnapped them detectives and let them live. Remember no body, no murder, no case." Larry pulled his cigar as he talked to Malachi.

"Larry, I don't plan on dying no time soon. So, fuck that cracker. He will be dead soon."

"That's why I like you, Malachi, you never back down. You and I both know you have the crown… shit, New York knows you have the crown. But the thing about the crown is once you are wearing it, you are not that hungry no more. So that cracker might just kill this nigga." Malachi looked at Larry and nodded, knowing he was telling the truth.

"So, you telling me to stand down?"

"No Malachi, like I said… no body, no murder, no case. Just because you are wearing the crown, don't mean a king can't bleed."

"I'ma go take care of the business now then."

"As I knew you would." Malachi didn't say a word as he walked off.

***

"Cordial, it's time you and Bishop find this pizza eating mother and close his eyes for good."

"Jazmine, don't nobody know where this motherfucker is at, we are looking for a ghost. Shit, we witch hunting right now."

"Cordial, I may know where to find Walter at and if worse comes to worse, we might just have to set up a meeting with him, then kill him." Bishop shook his head as he smoked on his blunt.

"Hell no, Malachi won't respect that, it will fuck his name up, hands down."

"We need to call Malachi, then Jazmine, because Bishop does have a point."

"Malachi is having a meeting with Larry, Kareem told me, so he's MIA right now."

"Look, fuck calling Malachi. Jazmine, you said you know where he might be?"

"Yeah."

"Good, get me the address and let's take care of the business, let's get this shit over with," Cordial said.

Jazmine pulled out her phone and handed it to him.

"There's the address, Cordial."

"Good, let's go."

***

"First, let me say I'm glad both of y'all are back in one piece. The whole police station was out there looking for y'all. I read both of y'all reports and trust me when I say this, I know y'all are damn good detectives, but as of 1:00 pm today, both of y'all are off the case. Before y'all say anything, this is above my pay grade. It came from up top." Captain Fuller looked at both detectives.

"Captain, you know this is some bullshit, we've been on this case for over a year and a half." Captain Fuller looked at Detective Benlose as he was talking.

"Detective, I said what I said, you're off the case. That will be all." Detective Benlose looked at Captain Fuller and got up and bit his bottom lip as he nodded his head and walked out of the office, with Detective Oldham behind him. Once out the door, Detective Benlose looked at Detective Oldham.

"Oldham, you know this is some bullshit taking us off the case like that."

"You know what, Benlose, I'm with the captain on this one. Fuck this mob shit, this war, Malachi, Walter. Bro, we could have been killed. Our families coulda been killed. And if my family or my wife and kids woulda got hurt behind this case, I couldn't live with myself. Captain said we are off the case, and that's all that matters to me."

"So, you are alright knowing this motherfucker could have killed your family or you?"

"But he didn't, we're still breathing and I'm not going to roll the dice by gambling with my family's lives. If Malachi wants to be the king, let him. This is a chess match now between Walter and Malachi and I'ma sit back and see who wins." Oldham patted Benlose on the back and walked off.

SAYNOMORE

Chapter 43

"Checkmate… life lesson, Tilmen. A pawn can kill a king if he in the right position. I see in your eyes your mind is made up. I see the fire that's burning in them. So, I'ma ask you one time, are you sure this is the life you want to live?" Tilmen looked up at Malachi and nodded.

"Come here, let me show you something. What you see when you look out this window?"

"People walking around, and cars."

"I see everybody that's going to want what you have soon. There's rules to this lifestyle, follow them and you will win, break them and you can get yourself killed." Rashad looked up at Malachi.

"What are the rules?"

"Rule one. Loyalty to yourself, before your family and the streets. You can rat on someone and never get caught. But you will know that you are a fucking rat. So, stay true to yourself. True to the game and the game will stay true to you. Two. Motherfuckers only respect violence. If they cross the line, kill them and whoever is standing with them, before that motherfucker is standin over your body holding a hot hammer in his hand.

"Three. If your family ain't healthy, then you ain't healthy. I don't care how much money you have, if they are broke, then you are broke. Four. Always know who you are dealing with. Just how I killed your king with a pawn, someone can kill you the same way. A brave man wins many fights, but a smart man wins them all. Five. Never walk in a man's shoes who is greater than you. You got that?"

"Yeah, I do."

"Tilmen, one day you are going to be standing where I am standing, and there's one thing I don't never want you to forget." Malachi looked down at Tilmen.

"What's that?"

"One day you might have to kill a friend, or a kid to get your point across. Don't let your heart fuck up what you already made up in your mind. Do what you have to do to win. Now come on, let's go get some pizza before I bring you home."

***

Detective Benlose watched as Jazmine got out of the car and walked into the hotel, he followed her on to the elevator. When she turned around the doors were closing, and he already had his gun pointed at her. He pressed the stop button on the elevator and put his gun to her head.

"Don't say a motherfucking word, bitch, I'll put your brains on that fucking wall behind you. Now fuck up and die." Jazmine closed her eyes and shook her head as Detective Benlose pressed the gun to the side of her head.

"Bitch, this ain't about you, it's about that fake ass big Meek nigga, Malachi. See, I'm the messenger, but you are going to be the motherfucking messenger. You tell that fake ass mob boss it ain't going to be no fucking trial, no plea deal. It's going to be one bullet, one bomb, one spark and one kill, when he fucked with my family, he crossed the line, now the boogie man is looking for him. Deliver the message, bitch."

Detective Benlose moved the gun from her face and pressed the button to open the elevator door. Jazmine looked at him as she bit her bottom lip. When he turned his back, she pulled her gun out of her purse and pointed at him as he stepped off the elevator.

"Yo, Detective." Detective Benlose turned around and looked at Jazmine as she had the gun pointed at him.

"Bitch, I ain't no message, I'm the fucking messenger." Jazmine pulled the trigger, shooting Detective Benlose three times in the chest. She watched as he fell backward on the floor and coughed up blood.

"News flash, pussy, that was me that took them pictures of your wife and kids. That was the warning, now this is the action behind it, boogie man." Jazmine shot Detective Benlose two times in the head before she ran out the lobby. Two people were watching the whole thing and within ten minutes, NYPD was down there at the hotel, everything was taped off.

Detective Oldham could not believe what he was seeing as he stood over Detective Benlose' dead body, knowing that they were just talking to each other a few hours ago. Now he's laying in a pool of blood with his eyes open and two holes in his head and three to his chest. A tear dropped from his eye as he looked at his friend when Captain Fuller walked up to him.

"I'm sorry about your friend, we checked and there are no cameras in this lobby. All we know at this time it was a female from what the witnesses are saying."

"A female?"

"Yea" Detective Oldham looked at Captain Fuller.

"Jazmine," he said as he walked away with hate in his heart.

***

Jazmine opened up the office door, breathing hard. Malachi and Kareem looked at her as she walked up to them.

"Jazmine, why are you breathing so hard, what happened?"

"Malachi, you remember Detective Benlose the one I took the pictures of?"

"Yeah."

"He caught me going to the hotel and ran up on me, gun out in the elevator, talking crazy. He had the gun to my face and all. Talking about killing me, you, and calling me all kinds of bitches—" Malachi cut Jazmine off.

"Jazmine, don't tell me what I know you are about to tell me."

"Malachi, I killed him. I shot him three times in the chest and two times in the head." Malachi took his hand and wiped it down his face as he took his fingers and was playing with the hair on his chin. Malachi licked his lips as he looked at Kareem.

"Kareem, put Jazmine on a private plane to South Carolina. We need her there within two hours from now, going into stores."

"Ok, I'm on it now. Jazmine, let's go." Jazmine looked at Malachi without saying a word, looking at Kareem as he walked out the door. Malachi knew Jazmine fucked up, but he also knew she was being loyal to the family.

SAYNOMORE

Chapter 44

Walking into the fish store, Walter looked around till he saw Lil John coming from the back. He walked up to him with a smile on his face.

"Walter, how long has it been?"

"Too long, you don't even look the same no more, you got ugly and old."

"Hey, when you have a wife like mine, you lose more than your hair and you drink a little more. So, let me guess, yo are here because of the heat that's coming down on all of us because of what this nigga is doing. Kidnapping and killing cops, that's just messy nigga shit."

"Yeah, I know. I'm sending my guys at him and his crew I'm ending this shit now."

"Good, because the one thing in our line of work is you live and die alone, and when you step in a great man's shoes, you will hang yourself. don't fuck that up, Walter." Walter nodded and walked off.

***

"What's the story we got on Detective Benlose' murder, what are the streets saying?" Captain Fuller looked at the chief.

"The streets ain't talking, but there was a kid playing with his mother's phone that got Detective Benlose on video with his gun in his hand, check it out." Captain Fuller passed the phone to the chief and watched how he reviewed the video.

"You have to be fucking kidding me. Who was the female he ran up to on the elevator, pointing his gun at?" Captain Fuller took a deep breath.

"Off the record, we think it's Jazmine from Malachi's crew, but we can't see her face so we don't know if it's her or not." The chief was still watching the video as Captain Fuller was talking.

"He let his guard down. She musta called his name, that's why he turned around. She shot him three times in the chest. Walked up to him, said something then she shot him two times in the head. The kid recorded everything from the back, that's why we can't see her face. Fuck, what was Detective Benlose thinking? And before, you said we, who is we?"

"Me and Detective Oldham believe strongly it's Jazmine."

"Believing strongly ain't proof. We need proof, that's it. Go make that happen for me, Captain, and I want to go over the reports this kid and mother made."

"Yes, sir." Captain Fuller got up and walked out of the Chief office. Once out the door, he pulled his phone out and dialed Detective Oldham's number. After a ring, Detective Oldham picked up.

"Detective Oldham, we need to talk, come to my office." After the captain said that he hung up the phone and walked off.

Chapter 45

Malachi walked with two of his guys to his car, not saying a word as he was deep in thought. Knowing Jazmine fucked up, he had to get her out of this somehow, and the beef with Walter was just more food on his plate to eat.

"Malachi, where are we going?"

"The 40's Projects, I need to see a friend."

"Sure thing, boss."

"You see them fucking niggas getting in the car, get ready, Walter wants them all fucking dead." The black Town Car rolled up on Malachi's car and rolled the windows down.

"Yoo, niggas." Malachi looked and saw the guns pointed at him. Before he could say a word, bullets were flying his way. He ducked down as bullets were coming through the car windows. Blood got all over Malachi as his driver was hit. He opened up the back door and jumped out of the car. He pulled his gun out and started shooting back. One of Walter's men jumped out of the car, shooting a Mac-11 at Malachi. Malachi's man looked up and pointed his gun at Walter's man, but before he could pull the trigger, he was shot two times in the chest, taking his life.

Malachi looked and shot Walter's man in the head, dropping him. That's when the car pulled off. Malachi ran to the street shooting at the car as it drove off, yelling, "You missed, motherfucker, you missed. I'm still here."

Malachi looked around at everyone coming outside looking at what was going on. Malachi put his gun up and walked back into the building and the crowd as he heard the police coming.

***

Bishop walked out the corner deal with Cordial when he got a page from Malachi.

"Cordial, Malachi just hit me on the hip with a 911 text, clap his line. Bro, real quick, shit must be real." Cordial pulled out his phone and called Malachi. Before Malachi could answer the phone, there was a white Fed-Ex truck coming down the street, with two men on the back of it, with Mac-11's shooting up the front of the store. Bullets were flying everywhere, breaking out the car windows, the front of the store window.

"Yo Bishop, Bishop. You good, bro?" Bishop was on the side of the car, holding his stomach.

"Y'all motherfuckers are dead, on God, pussy." Cordial jumped from the side of the car shooting at both men with guns in each hand. He didn't see the other man on the side of the truck coming from behind with his gun in his hand. As Cordial was shooting, Walter's man ran up behind him and was about to shoot him, when Bishop jumped from behind the car grabbing him.

"You dumb nigga, now you are going to die," Walter's man said as he looked into Bishop eyes. He took his gun and pressed it to his stomach. Bishop looked at Cordial, who was still shooting at Walter's men. When he felt the bullets going through his stomach, he looked at Walter's man as blood started coming out his mouth. Walter's man let Bishop go as his body hit the ground. Cordial turned around and looked at Bishop's body on the ground in a pool of blood. He started to shoot at Walter's man as he was running away.

Back at the truck, Cordial ran to Bishop as the truck drove off and laid his gun down next to Bishop as he held his hand and head up. Bishop was trying to talk as blood came out his mouth.

"Don't say nothing, man. You good, we are going to get you some help. I got you, bro." Cordial looked around as he was yelling for help when Bishop said his name.

"Cordial."

"Yeah, man, I'm right here."

"I stopped him, I saw him was watching you blind side bro."

"I love you, bro. it's over, man, my body is cold."

"You going to make it bro, we are going to be laughing about this in a few days." Cordial looked at Bishop as he took his last breath, dying in his arms. Cordial laid Bishop's head down on the ground and took his hand and closed his eyes. He picked his gun up and got up, getting into his car and driving off before the police came.

Chapter 46

Walter smoked his cigar as he looked out the back window at the lake at his house. He wanted to show Malachi who the fuck he was, and that no nigga was gone to pump fear into his heart. Walter pulled his cigar as his phone started to ring, he turned around and walked to the table and picked the phone up.

"Hello," Walter said as he sat down on the edge of the table.

"Boss, Malachi and his crew of niggas got hit."

"Good, real good. Now, that nigga knows who he is playing with?" Walter hung up the phone and walked back to the window as he looked back at the lake with the sun reflection glowing on it.

***

Malachi hung up the phone and threw the bottle of brandy against the wall and kicked over one of the chairs in his office as Kareem looked at him.

"Malachi, keep your cool." Malachi turned around and looked at Kareem.

"That was Cordial, he said they just killed Bishop down on 114th at the deli."

"Fuck, man, we need to make a move and make it now."

"Kareem, these noodle eating motherfuckers crossed the wrong line, the gloves is off, everything is fair game now. Find out where his wife and kids stay. I'ma hurt this motherfucker and in a way, he will never be able to bounce back from. If he wants a war, I'll make it rain shells. World War III just popped off.

SAYNOMORE

Chapter 47

Malachi placed a red rose down on Bishop's chest, then he rested his hand on top of his.

"You ain't going to die alone. I promise you that, Bishop. I promise you that." Malachi turned around and walked out of the church, where he had five of his men on guard, waiting on him out front. As the church doors closed, Malachi saw Detective Oldham walking up to him. He pulled out his cigar and lit it as Detective Oldham walked up to him.

"Malachi, I know just your words can get someone killed, and it might've been you who had me and Detective Benlose kidnapped, but still stand here in front of you. I'm not afraid to die. Malachi, hear me clearly. You win. I'm done." Detective Oldham looked around, then reached into his jacket and pulled out a yellow folder with a thumb drive taped to it, and handed it to Malachi.

"Like I said, I'm done. I just want to live my life now in peace." Malachi looked at the folder and nodded. Detective Oldham nodded back and turned around and walked away.

"You see what the fuck happened when yo run your block. Even the boys in blue respect who the fuck I am. Now come on, we got some noodle eating motherfuckers to kill."

***

Malachi looked around at the table at everyone that was there. He looked at Bishop's seat, empty. He closed his eyes and shook his head.

"It's time for shit to go boom, I want bodies in the streets. Cordial, I want that fat, noodle eating motherfucker to know what it is like to get your heart ripped out of your chest." Malachi looked at Cordial with hate in his eyes. Cordial returned the same look.

"Cordial, I want his wife, son, and daughter. Everybody in the fucking house dead. I want every fucking soul to leave out every fucking body in there."

"The shit I'ma do in that house is going to bring me more joy than a Christmas fucking morning, Malachi."

"Good, I can't wait to read about it." At that time everybody looked at the office door as it opened, and Jazmine walked inside.

"Jazmine, what are you doing here?" Jazmine walked up to Malachi.

"I have every fucking right to be here. Bishop is just not your brother, but mines too and when his blood got spilled, they spilled mines too." Jazmine looked Malachi dead in the eyes.

Malachi nodded.

"Take your seat, Jazmine." Jazmine sat next to Kareem.

"Cordial, you have the address to Walter's house thanks to Detective Oldham."

"Wait. I'm lost, Malachi. Detective Oldham is with us now?" Jazmine said.

"No, after you killed Detective Benlose, you shook him up. So, in good faith, he brings me all Walter's information, your video of you killing Detective Benlose. Just for a pass for him and his family."

"Whoa, ok, but do you trust the information?"

"Cordial already been by there two times. We was just waiting for Bishop's funeral to be over before we pop the bottle."

"Ok, now let's go catch some bodies."

"Jazmine, you and Kareem will go kill Walter." Kareem called Malachi's name.

"Malachi, we don't even know where this motherfucker be at, and the only reason his wife and kids are at the house is because of mob laws, no one could touch a man's family at war."

"That's the thing, Kareem, we ain't the fucking mob so fuck their laws. We play by our own rules and break them bitches when we get ready. Like I said, every noodle eating motherfucker you see, kill them." Malachi watched as everyone got up from the table and walked out the office.

"Jazmine?"

"Yes, Malachi?"

"Welcome home."

154

"Thanks, it's good to be home." Jazmine walked up to Malachi and kissed his cheek before leaving the office.

SAYNOMORE

Chapter 48

"I don't care about your tears, bitch, or how old this little nigga is. You know what the fuck you signed up for when you said I do. News flash, bitch, you and your son is the message for your coward ass husband." Cordial's heart was cold as he poured gas all over Walter's wife and son as they were tied up on the floor. He pulled his phone out and bent down and took the tape off of Walter's wife and son's mouths.

"Whatever you want to say to your husband, say it now because you will be dead in five more minutes." Cordial set his phone up on the floor as it recorded Walter's wife crying as she pleaded for her and her son's life. Cordial poured more gas on them as his phone recorded everything.

"Baby, please come save us, please come home. Walter, they are going to kill us. I don't want to die." Cordial lit a match and dropped it on her. Her and her son let out a loud scream as they were being burned alive and Cordial recorded it all. He picked up his phone and walked out the house.

***

Malachi walked to his sound system and played Marvin Gaye and Tammi Terrell's "Ain't No Mountain High Enough." He started bopping his head to the music as he lit his cigar, singing along to the song, knowing his team was putting in the work tonight.

"Listen, baby. Ain't no mountain high enough, ain't no valley low enough, ain't no river wide enough, baby. If you need me, call me. no matter where you are, no matter how far no worries baby. Just call my name. Just call my name. I'll be there in a hurry, you don't have to worry, because there ain't no mountain high enough ain't no valley low enough, ain't no river wide enough, to keep me from getting to you, baby. Malachi sat on his desk and pulled his cigar, knowing his messenge was being delivered.

***

"You ready, Jazmine?"

"Yeah, let's do this." Jazmine put her murder one mask on and cocked her two guns back and nodded at Kareem. Kareem ran up and kicked the pool hall door open. Jazmine ran in behind him, shooting both .45 Colts as Kareem let off the M-16. Shooting up the bar and everything around it as Jazmine shot up the pool tables, people were tripping over dead bodies as they were running.

"Come on, come on… it's time to get the fuck up out of here before them boys come," Kareem yelled.

Jazmine looked down at one of the dead Italians as she pointed her gun at his face and fired two times, before running out the pool hall. As she got in the car, Walter's man ran to the door, shooting at the car as it drove off.

Chapter 49

"No-no-no, who the fuck was guarding the house? My wife, my son! Jesus, no." Walter sat on the bench as he had his hand over his face in his backyard, while the police were walking around his burned-down house with his wife and son on the inside.

"Walter, Lue and Eddie were here, but whoever did this got to them too." Walter looked up at Steve and stood up in front of him.

"Whoever did this, you said? Me and you both know this nigga is behind this. Say one word and I'll have your head chopped the fuck off. My fucking wife and son is in there burned to death, and you said whoever did this? Get the fuck away from me before you find yourself dead, now!" Walter watched as Steve walked off.

"No father should have to come home to a dead child, or husband to a dead wife. I want this nigga killed and skinned alive. How the fuck did he know where I live?" Walter looked as they were carrying his wife and son out the house in body bags.

"Come on, I have to get out of here."

***

"Malachi, can I ask you something?" Malachi looked at Rashad as he sat in the chair in front of his desk, with his black hoodie on black jeans and black Timberland boots on. Malachi ran his finger down his cheek to his chin.

"What's on your mind? Speak it."

"I been watching the news with my mom and the lady on the news said this mob war with Malachi Williams and Walter Gambino is very deadly, and she also said because of this war Walter Gambino's family, his wife and son were killed, they were tied up and burned alive. She ain't say you did it, but that's the word that is going around. I want to know did you kill them that way?" Malachi lit his cigar and pulled it before talking.

"Rashad, sometimes you have to do things you don't want to, but you have to. Sometimes talking ain't enough. In today's world, people only respect violence. It's a dog-eat-dog world. There are two types of respect in this world. People respect you for who you are. That's the first one. And the second one, they respect you because they fear you because they know what you are capable of doing. You asked me did I kill them? No, I didn't kill them but the right question you shoulda asked me. Did I get them killed?"

"Did you?" Malachi pulled his cigar and blew the smoke out.

"Yeah, I did, it was necessary. His family was collateral damage. Now, come on, it's your move on the chessboard. And Rashad, never ask me about the family business again." Rashad nodded.

Chapter 50

Walter's limo pulled up to the East River, where Larry and David were waiting on him, with their guards standing around. Walter got out of the limo and walked up to both men and shook their hands.

"Larry. You and David, thank you for seeing me on a short notice like this one."

"No problem, Walter, what can we do for you?"

"My wife is dead, my son is dead, burned alive. I couldn't bear to look at the bodies like that, and this nigga Malachi has no heart. Who kills a man's family? I mean, the five-year-old son… you just don't do that, there are laws and rules you have to go by."

"Walter, just like I told you at the service, I am deeply sorry for your loss, but Malachi don't have to follow no laws. He is not in the mob. He was Washington's toy puppet. Now he is his own man. But my question to you is, what can we do for you? Why did you want to meet us today?" Walter took a deep breath.

"I need your help to kill the nigga. I want him dead in the worst way. I'm asking for your help today. I'm ready to put my blood on the contract today for your help."

"If you put your blood on the contract, I own you and I want twenty percent of everything you make, and you will be on call when I call you." Walter looked at Larry and David and took the knife out of his pocket and cut his hand, then placed it on a piece of paper with his name on it. Larry did the same thing.

"I'll take care of Malachi. You be ready when I call you."

"I'll be ready." Walter turned around and walked back to his limo and got inside. Larry watched as it drove off.

"Larry, you work with Malachi."

"I did work with Malachi, now our season have ended. Malachi did everything I needed him to do to put me where I needed to be again. He killed Washington, Lee, Grunt, and Peter. He took over Brooklyn. I'm the puppet master and Malachi was my puppet. I don't need him no more. Plus, how long did you think I was going to have that nigga around, when you have good pure Italian blood that can do everything Malachi can do for me, maybe even better.

And think about this, David, he killed Washington… someone who helped him get where he is today. The nigga have no loyalty, so fuck him."

"Larry, you make a good point, but killing Malachi might not be as easy as you think."

"You right, it's going to be easier, David." David nodded as they both got in the limo and drove off.

***

"Calvin, I want you and Robert to have someone take care of Malachi. I have to agree with Walter about this nigga. At first, I liked him, but now he's just getting in the way. He needs to take a trip that he will not come back from." Calvin took a sip of his drink as he lit his cigar.

"Killing Malachi is not the problem. It's the fucking domino effect that's going to come after it. There's been cop killings, body droppings. The city is on fire, Larry, you backed up a nigga. Now the damn newspaper is calling him Mr. Untouchable." Calvin pulled his cigar and looked at Larry.

"So now, my question to you, Calvin. Now that you know what I need done, can I count on you to get it done? You know how much I hate to be disappointed, Calvin." Larry walked up to Calvin and placed a phone down on the table.

"This is a clean line. Call me when I'm done." Calvin picked up the phone and looked at it before putting it in his pocket.

"I'll be in touch." Larry smiled as he lowered his head and lit his cigar.

"Good. Do I have to put a timeline on this, or can I trust it will be done in a fashionable time?"

"You can trust it will get done, Larry."

"That's the thing about trust, it goes both ways. I trust you will get it done, but the question is, do you trust you can get it done?" Larry walked out of the pool hall after saying what he said.

Chapter 51

"Is Walter inside?" The guard turned around and nodded his head at Walter's office door.

"Let me tell you now, Green. Someone sent him a video of his son and wife being burned alive, he's not too good back there, just a heads up."

"Thanks." Green walked to the door and opened it up and looked at Walter as he sat behind his desk with tears in his eyes as he looked at his family as they were being burned alive screaming for his help calling out his name. He shook his head and looked up at Walter. He placed his phone face down and took a shot of gin.

"What kind of man kills a young boy who don't even have hair on his nuts? Green, they burnt my boy alive, then sent me the video. Who does this to a man? Where was the fucking honor in him. Green, I want this nigga dead. Dead!"

"I promise you Walter I will kill this nigga in the worst way and everyone around him will die screaming." Walter walked around the desk and placed both his hands on Green's face and looked him in the eyes.

"Green, if you find this nigga and kill him, I will make you a made man and my number two. I swear on the blood of my father" Green grabbed Walter's hands and moved them from his face and kissed them two times.

"I swear, I won't let you down, Walter."

"I know you won't." Green kissed his hands one more time before walking off.

***

"Malachi, Walter got the video. You know what you did by showing him that?"

"Yeah, I do. I'ma bring him the only thing that's going to give him the hate he has for me to come out of hiding. You know how you kill a boss?"

"You catch him down bad, Malachi, and you let someone else find the body."

"No, Kareem. When you kill a boss, you don't do it in the dark. You kill him where the whole city can watch him die, and that's how Walter will die, where the whole city can watch." Kareem smiled as he picked up his glass of brandy and took a sip.

"You are a cold-hearted motherfucker, Malachi."

"No. I just do what I need to do to get my point across, no matter what it takes."

"So, what's the plan?"

"Set the bait and let him come to me. Let the wolf think he's the predator when he really is the prey." Malachi stopped talking when Jazmine walked into the room with Cordial.

"How are we looking out there?" Jazmine sat down at the table and placed her gun on top of it.

"Ain't nobody around right now. The blocks are empty, no police, no noodle eating motherfuckers, just some crack heads and street walkers."

"Malachi, check me out. We hit all of Walter's spots, killed his family in the worst way, laid his hittas down. He ain't trying to come back he know what time it is."

"Walter is strong willed, very respected, he's going to come back, Cordial."

"So, let's strike first again, but this time harder."

"Cordial, it's not about the first move but the last move." Malachi walked to the table and picked up his stress balls and looked at Kareem.

"Burn the pool hall down and everything he owns till he comes at us."

"Say less, homie, I'm on it."

Chapter 52

"Walter, word just got back to me that Malachi is on Main Street at the pizza joint." Walter looked at Green with hate in his eyes. He got up off the bar stool with his gun in his hand.

"Get the boys, it's time to go kill a nigga." Walter and his guys walked out the pool hall to their cars.

***

"Malachi, it's crazy we out here on Walter's blocks like this in the open." Malachi smiled as he walked out the pizza spot with Kareem and Jazmine by his side.

"Fuck Walter. I want him to come at us and Kareem, these are my fucking blocks now." Walter watched as Malachi walked out of the pizza spot. He pulled his gun out and nodded at his driver. Malachi looked as the black Town Car was headed his way. He watched as the gun was hanging out the window pointing at him. He jumped in front of Jazmine and pulled his gun out.

"Get right, get right, it's go time," Malachi yelled as he started shooting at the black Town Car. Jazmine took off running behind a parked car as she pulled her gun out. Gunshots sounded off everywhere. Malachi looked back and saw Kareem laying on his back.

"Malachi, on the blood of my son, you are a dead nigga." Walter jumped out the car shooting at Malachi, people were running and recording everything with their cell phones. Malachi was ducked behind a pickup truck as he waited for Walter to get up closer to him. Once Malachi saw his feet, he jumped from behind the pickup truck and punched Walter in the face. Then he knocked his gun out of his hand as Walter took two steps back. He wiped the blood from his mouth and spit on the ground. Walter looked at his guys on the ground dead, then at Jazmine holding the gun in her hand.

"See, it's just you and me now, motherfucker. Your men are dead and soon you will be too."

"Do you think I will let a nigga take my life, a fried chicken eating motherfucker?" Walter pulled a switch blade out of his pocket and started walking towards Malachi. Malachi looked around at everyone with their phones out recording everything. Malachi threw his hands up as Walter swung the knife at Malachi. Malachi moved out the way, Walter swung it again and Malachi blocked it with his arm. Walter cut him.

"Nigga blood. I love the sight of it." Malachi bit down on his teeth and rushed Walter and grabbed him and turned him around and put him in the head lock as he choked him out. Walter was fighting too. He was going unconscious, and he dropped the knife out of his hand as Malachi continued to choke him till Walter wasn't moving at all.

Malachi heard the police sirens coming his way. He dropped Walter, then took Walter's knife and ran it across his face, giving Walter a buck-fifty across the face. He took off to where Kareem was laying on the ground. Malachi and Jazmine picked him up, got him in the car and drove off as the police were coming down the block.

Chapter 53

"Walter, you could have been killed, what were you thinking?" Walter couldn't stop looking in the mirror at the cut on his face as Green was talking to him.

"You took three guys and one car to go kill Malachi, two got killed in the car and one as he stepped out of the car. If the police ain't come when they did, you would have been a dead man, be grateful they were on your payroll."

"Green, this nigga could have killed me, and I will put every motherfucker in the line of fire till this nigga is dead. Look at my fucking face, look at it." Green knew that Walter wasn't in his right state of mind. He loved the Gambino family and didn't want to see it burn down because of Walter and his hate for Malachi.

"I'll be back, boss. I'm going to check on the guys." Walter didn't say a word, he just kept looking in the mirror.

***

"I don't remember nothing, just gunshots, then tripping and hitting my head on the curb."

"I took his soul from him in front of everyone, his respect, his fear, everyone knows that Walter Gambino can bleed now." Malachi walked to the bar and poured him and Kareem a drink. He sat down at the table after he gave Kareem his glass.

"So, what now, Malachi?" Malachi lit his cigar and blew the smoke out of his mouth. Before Malachi could answer, there was a knock at his office door. Kareem looked at Malachi, Malachi placed his gun on the table and nodded at Kareem to open the door. Kareem got up and walked to the door and opened it to see David and two of his men standing there.

"Let them in, Kareem." Malchi got up and walked to David and shook his hand.

"Please, come have a seat. Can I get you something to drink?"

"Yeah, that would be nice" Malachi got a bottle of brandy and a glass and walked to the table and took his seat.

"So, tell me what brings you by?" David took a deep breath. "Let's share a cigar before we have this conversation."

Malachi nodded and reached in his pocket and pulled out a cigar for David and handed it to him.

"Malachi, you are very respected, but hated even more and you know this already. Don't you?"

"Yeah, I do, and if they don't respect me the way I want them to, then they will fear me the way they don't want to." Malachi placed his hand on his chin as he waited for David to tell him why he is really there.

"Malachi, I'ma get to the point of this visit. Larry is not your friend, he ain't even on your side. He signed a contract with Walter to have you killed."

"With no disrespect, why should I believe this? Larry helped me get where I am today."

"You right, why should you believe me? After all he's done for you?" Malachi took a sip of his brandy.

"Let's say this is true, why are you going against him for me?"

"I have my own reason for that but let me show you something."

David slid Malachi the contract with Larry and Walter's blood on it. Malachi placed his drink down on the table and looked at David.

"Malachi, kill Larry and I will supply you with whatever you need, and you will always have a friend in me." Malachi handed David back the contract and looked at Kareem.

"I'll get it done."

"I know you will. Malachi, trust no one and thanks for the cigar and drink." David got up and walked out Malachi's office, leaving him in his thoughts.

Chapter 54

Larry looked at David as he waited for him by the limo, with two of his men. He lit his cigar and started walking to them. David walked off from both men and walked up to Larry.

"Where is this meeting at with Malachi?"

"Down at Corrections Pool Hall on the east side, but we are not having a meeting, we are going to see an assassination, David," Larry said with a smile.

"Who is doing the job?"

"Green, and if he misses his shot tonight, then Calvin and Robert will take care of their shot. Malachi has become too comfortable. He forgot the number one rule in the mob, trust no one. Now come, let's not be late for the show." David nodded as he followed Larry to the limo.

***

"Malachi, you are talking about killing David and Larry. That's both plugs. How are we going to eat behind this?"

"Kareem, Larry and David been flying too close to the sun lately. Sometimes you win, even when you lose. Larry wants to see me in a pine box and if David crossed him out, why the fuck do he care about a nigga? We are going to take the loss and win at the same time." Malachi looked at everyone at the table, before addressing them all.

"We play with the hand we are dealt. We take on all contenders, that's how life works. Stupid is knowing the truth but still believing the lie. Larry fucked up by crossing me. He thinks when it comes to me and him, I'm not a threat, but I'm the fucking predator and that what makes me more dangerous. When Larry's car pulls up to the pool hall, don't nobody give him a chance to get out. I want him killed before he can step out of the car and everyone who is with him. Cordial, you will take the kill shot on Larry, he will be on the right side back seat. Jazmine, you will kill David. Tru, you will kill the driver when the car pulls up. You know the drill, shoot or get shot. Come on, let's get this done."

Malachi and Kareem sat in the car across the street and watched as Larry's car pulled up. Malachi leaned forward as Larry's car stopped. Malachi watched as Larry's door opened, he stepped out of the car, smoking a cigar. He didn't see Cordial coming from behind him to it was too late. Back-to-back gunshots were heard as Tru and Jazmine were also shooting, and you saw all three men laying in pools of blood. Kareem started the car up and drove past slowly to make sure all three men were dead. Malachi nodded and pulled his cigar as he rode past them.

Chapter 55

"Larry is dead, so is David. The question is, do you really want to go to Malachi? He already showed us he can stand toe to toe with the best. Calvin, I'm telling you now just walk away, it's too late. Walter, his mind is made up already and his pride will get him killed, so I'm telling you now to walk away." Calvin looked at Lil John and nodded.

"And what are we going to do about Malachi?"

"Let Walter and Malachi kill each other, then we will pick-up the breadcrumbs they leave behind. How their story ends is in prison and a grave, the question is who is going where." Lil John pulled his cigar and smiled at Calvin.

"What about Larry and David, we just going to let they murder go unanswered?"

"Word got around that Larry took up the contract on Malachi for Walter for a blood price, and it got him and David killed. Now the big question is, who told Malachi? How did he find out about this contract?" Calvin picked up his glass and took a sip.

"And who gets Brooklyn when the wolves kill each other and leave the mess in the streets?"

"Whoever wants to clean up the mess out there."

"So be it, then. There is nothing else to talk about then, let's see the outcome of this horror movie we been watching for the last two and a half years."

"Yes, let's see how it ends." Lil John tapped his cigar against Calvin's glass as both men nodded to their agreement.

***

"Malachi, it's over, Walter sent you a white rose with blood on it." Malachi walked to the box on the table and looked at the rose in the box as he picked it up.

"The white rose is for the innocent and the blood is for the pain we cause their loved ones. This don't mean it's over. It just means he needs time to get things back in order."

"So, we need to strike him now while he is down. This is the best time." Malachi placed the rose back in the box and looked at Kareem.

"Kareem, know when to claim your victory and when to walk away. Kareem, in victory, know when to stop after you reach your mark. This ain't over, it's just the beginning, Kareem."

"So, what are we going to do about the plug, now we need a new one? We may have enough work to get us by for the next few months, then what?"

Malachi lit his cigar and walked to his office window and looked out, and saw a black limo pull up. He pulled on his cigar and turned around and looked at Kareem, then walked to the bar and got two glasses and a bottle of Cîroc lime and placed it on the table in a bucket of ice. Within two minutes, the office door opened up and all eyes was on the female standing in the doorway, looking at her long honey-brown hair, hazy eyes caramel skin and hourglass body.

Kareem knew this female was a boss bitch and she was about her business, he could tell she was strong-willed, bold, focused and dangerous. She cut her eyes at Kareem then back at Malachi as she walked up to Malachi and shook his hand. Both her bodyguards stood at the door with a murderous look in their eyes.

"Jamila Lacross, it's finally good to meet the queen of New York City, the boss of all bosses."

"Likewise, it's good to meet you too, Malachi Williams. I heard so much about you." Malachi couldn't help but to look into her eyes as he looked at the angel of death in front of him.

"Please, come have a seat at the table so we can talk." Jamila walked past Kareem and took a seat at the table next to Malachi. Kareem heard many stories about Jamila, aka Red Invee, and the body count she leaves behind. He knew if she was there for Malachi, there was no place Malachi could go but up, and more bodies to be identified in New York City streets. To be the King, it comes with a price and in both of their cases, it was a blood price and they both lived by the same law, shoot or get shot.

***

Walter sat behind this desk, reading the newspaper about Larry and David's murder, as he drank his coffee and smoked his cigar. The headlines read, *The Boss is Dead*, with pictures of Larry and David outside the car in front of the pool hall in a pool of blood. He read in the paper about the murder of mobster godfather, Larry Bonanno. *Slain Mob Chief and Two Others Die in Gang War.* There were pictures of all three men on the front page. When he looked up, Green was walking in the office door.

"Would you believe this shit? it's just like this nigga just don't want to die, and don't nobody but me want to do shit about it. Yellow pants ass thugs." Walter placed the paper down on his desk and leaned back in his seat.

"So, tell me what you got." Green sat in front of Walter's desk and crossed his legs as he rested his hand on his chin.

"Within the last two and a half years, Peter and Lee, Washington and Grunt, Larry and David, now the other families wanted to put an end to this ongoing war. Walter, no one is going to aid and assist us on this. Lil John said accept the loss on your family. It comes in this life we live. Calvin and Robert said the same thing, no one is backing us up on this." Walter got up and walked to the window and looked out of it.

"How do you feel about us just walking away?"

"The real question is, how do *you* feel about it?"

"I watched the video of my son and wife being burnt alive over and over again. You asked me how I feel. Let me tell you how I feel, like a man who lost his family, my fucking heart was ripped out. You right, this ain't mob shit, this is fucking personal, and I won't stop till I have his head on a fucking pike. That's how the fuck I feel, Green."

"So, what about us?"

"This ain't about y'all, this is about two kings on one chess board and in chess, pawns die and one king lives. That should answer your question."

"So, we are expendable to you? Kill the men who killed your family."

"Y'all know what you signed up for when you walked through that door."

"And you know what you signed up for too, that's why your family is dead."

"Son of a bitch!" Walter turned around fast and was looking in the eye of a black 9mm with a silencer on it.

"So, they sent you to kill me? Who was it, Lil John? Calvin? Robert?"

"Does it matter?"

"Fuck you and all of yo nigga lovers. Bury me shallow because I'll be back."

"No, you won't." Green shot Walter three times in the chest, dropping him. Then one more time in the head, confirming the kill before walking out the office.

Chapter 56

Green stepped out of the car and walked up to Calvin and Lil John, as they stood next to the burned down car in the junkyard. He walked up to them and shook their hands.

"Green, it's good to see you. So, I'm thinking Walter is with his family as of last night?" Green looked at Lil John.

"The business is taken care of. Walter is dead. His mind was made up. He didn't care who had to die or what it took to kill Malachi." Calvin nodded and picked up the bag by his foot and handed it to Green. Green opened up the bag and was looking at the money. Lil John looked up and nodded as Green was counting the money. That's when the shot rang out. Green's body hit the ground, Calvin took a step close to Green and picked up the bag of money.

"So, what are you going to do with the body?"

"What body?" Lil John stepped over Green's body as his guys put his body in the trunk of the burned down car.

"You are right, Lil John, what body?" Both men started to laugh as they made their way to their cars.

***

"Did you just get all that on film, Alexis?"

"Yeah, Adam I did. Why they just kill Green you think?"

"That's a hell of a question. A better question is, who killed Walter, because of what we've just seen. We know Malachi Williams' hands are clean."

"Do you think Lil John and Calvin killed both of them to stop this mob war?"

"What I think is there is going to be a new boss. The question is, who is going to take over the Bonanno family? But what we just got on film in due time, we will find out because of the conversation we are going to have with Calvin Reeves and John Schott. Because right now we got the ball in our court, so we ask the questions, and we end the conversation with deal or no deal. Now, come on, let's show the captain what we got."

To Be Continued…
The Black Diamond Cartel 2
Coming Soon

Lock Down Publications and Ca$h Presents assisted publishing packages.

BASIC PACKAGE $499
Editing
Cover Design
Formatting

UPGRADED PACKAGE $800
Typing
Editing
Cover Design
Formatting

ADVANCE PACKAGE $1,200
Typing
Editing
Cover Design
Formatting
Copyright registration
Proofreading
Upload book to Amazon

LDP SUPREME PACKAGE $1,500
Typing
Editing
Cover Design
Formatting
Copyright registration
Proofreading
Set up Amazon account
Upload book to Amazon
Advertise on LDP Amazon and Facebook page

***Other services available upon request. Additional charges
may apply
Lock Down Publications
P.O. Box 944
Stockbridge, GA 30281-9998
Phone # 470 303-9761

Submission Guideline

Submit the first three chapters of your completed manuscript to ldpsubmissions@gmail.com, subject line: Your book's title. The manuscript must be in a .doc file and sent as an attachment. Document should be in Times New Roman, double spaced and in size 12 font. Also, provide your synopsis and full contact information. If sending multiple submissions, they must each be in a separate email.

Have a story but no way to send it electronically? You can still submit to LDP/Ca$h Presents. Send in the first three chapters, written or typed, of your completed manuscript to:

LDP: Submissions Dept
Po Box 944
Stockbridge, Ga 30281

DO NOT send original manuscript. Must be a duplicate.

Provide your synopsis and a cover letter containing your full contact information.

Thanks for considering LDP and Ca$h Presents.

SAYNOMORE

NEW RELEASES

THE COCAINE PRINCESS 9 by KING RIO

FOR THE LOVE OF BLOOD 3 by JAMEL MITCHELL

SANCTIFIED AND HORNY by XTASY

THE PLUG OF LIL MEXICO 2 by CHRIS GREEN

THE BLACK DIAMOND CARTEL by SAYNOMORE

The Black Diamond Cartel

SAYNOMORE

STRAIGHT BEAST MODE III

De'Kari

KINGPIN KILLAZ IV

STREET KINGS III

PAID IN BLOOD III

CARTEL KILLAZ IV

DOPE GODS III

Hood Rich

SINS OF A HUSTLA II

ASAD

YAYO V

Bred In The Game 2

S. Allen

THE STREETS WILL TALK II

By Yolanda Moore

SON OF A DOPE FIEND III

HEAVEN GOT A GHETTO III

SKI MASK MONEY III

By Renta

LOYALTY AIN'T PROMISED III

By Keith Williams

I'M NOTHING WITHOUT HIS LOVE II

SINS OF A THUG II

TO THE THUG I LOVED BEFORE II

IN A HUSTLER I TRUST II

By Monet Dragun

QUIET MONEY IV

EXTENDED CLIP III

THUG LIFE IV

By **Trai'Quan**

The Black Diamond Cartel

THE STREETS MADE ME IV

By **Larry D. Wright**

IF YOU CROSS ME ONCE III

ANGEL V

By **Anthony Fields**

THE STREETS WILL NEVER CLOSE IV

By **K'ajji**

HARD AND RUTHLESS III

KILLA KOUNTY IV

By **Khufu**

MONEY GAME III

By **Smoove Dolla**

JACK BOYS VS DOPE BOYS IV

A GANGSTA'S QUR'AN V

COKE GIRLZ II

COKE BOYS II

LIFE OF A SAVAGE V

CHI'RAQ GANGSTAS V

SOSA GANG IV

BRONX SAVAGES II

BODYMORE KINGPINS II

BLOOD OF A GOON II

By **Romell Tukes**

MURDA WAS THE CASE III

Elijah R. Freeman

AN UNFORESEEN LOVE IV

BABY, I'M WINTERTIME COLD III

By **Meesha**

QUEEN OF THE ZOO III

SAYNOMORE

By **Black Migo**

CONFESSIONS OF A JACKBOY III

By Nicholas Lock

KING KILLA II

By Vincent "Vitto" Holloway

BETRAYAL OF A THUG III

By Fre$h

THE BIRTH OF A GANGSTER III

By Delmont Player

TREAL LOVE II

By Le'Monica Jackson

FOR THE LOVE OF BLOOD IV

By Jamel Mitchell

RAN OFF ON DA PLUG II

By Paper Boi Rari

HOOD CONSIGLIERE III

By Keese

PRETTY GIRLS DO NASTY THINGS II

By Nicole Goosby

LOVE IN THE TRENCHES II

By Corey Robinson

FOREVER GANGSTA III

By Adrian Dulan

THE COCAINE PRINCESS X

SUPER GREMLIN II

By King Rio

CRIME BOSS II

Playa Ray

LOYALTY IS EVERYTHING III

Molotti

The Black Diamond Cartel

HERE TODAY GONE TOMORROW II
By Fly Rock
REAL G'S MOVE IN SILENCE II
By Von Diesel
GRIMEY WAYS IV
By Ray Vinci
SALUTE MY SAVAGERY II
By Fumiya Payne
BLOOD AND GAMES II
By King Dream
THE BLACK DIAMOND CARTEL II
By SayNoMore

<u>Available Now</u>

RESTRAINING ORDER **I & II**
By **CA$H & Coffee**
LOVE KNOWS NO BOUNDARIES **I II & III**
By **Coffee**
RAISED AS A GOON I, II, III & IV
BRED BY THE SLUMS I, II, III
BLAST FOR ME I & II
ROTTEN TO THE CORE I II III
A BRONX TALE I, II, III
DUFFLE BAG CARTEL I II III IV V VI

SAYNOMORE

HEARTLESS GOON I II III IV V

A SAVAGE DOPEBOY I II

DRUG LORDS I II III

CUTTHROAT MAFIA I II

KING OF THE TRENCHES

By **Ghost**

LAY IT DOWN **I & II**

LAST OF A DYING BREED I II

BLOOD STAINS OF A SHOTTA I & II III

By **Jamaica**

LOYAL TO THE GAME I II III

LIFE OF SIN I, II III

By **TJ & Jelissa**

BLOODY COMMAS I & II

SKI MASK CARTEL I II & III

KING OF NEW YORK I II,III IV V

RISE TO POWER I II III

COKE KINGS I II III IV V

BORN HEARTLESS I II III IV

KING OF THE TRAP I II

By **T.J. Edwards**

IF LOVING HIM IS WRONG…I & II

LOVE ME EVEN WHEN IT HURTS I II III

By **Jelissa**

WHEN THE STREETS CLAP BACK I & II III

THE HEART OF A SAVAGE I II III IV

MONEY MAFIA I II

LOYAL TO THE SOIL I II III

By **Jibril Williams**

A DISTINGUISHED THUG STOLE MY HEART I II & III

The Black Diamond Cartel

LOVE SHOULDN'T HURT I II III IV

RENEGADE BOYS I II III IV

PAID IN KARMA I II III

SAVAGE STORMS I II III

AN UNFORESEEN LOVE I II III

BABY, I'M WINTERTIME COLD I II

By **Meesha**

A GANGSTER'S CODE I &, II III

A GANGSTER'S SYN I II III

THE SAVAGE LIFE I II III

CHAINED TO THE STREETS I II III

BLOOD ON THE MONEY I II III

A GANGSTA'S PAIN I II III

By J-Blunt

PUSH IT TO THE LIMIT

By **Bre' Hayes**

BLOOD OF A BOSS **I, II, III, IV, V**

SHADOWS OF THE GAME

TRAP BASTARD

By **Askari**

THE STREETS BLEED MURDER **I, II & III**

THE HEART OF A GANGSTA I II& III

By **Jerry Jackson**

CUM FOR ME I II III IV V VI VII VIII

An **LDP Erotica Collaboration**

BRIDE OF A HUSTLA **I II & II**

THE FETTI GIRLS **I, II& III**

CORRUPTED BY A GANGSTA I, II III, IV

BLINDED BY HIS LOVE

THE PRICE YOU PAY FOR LOVE I, II ,III

SAYNOMORE

DOPE GIRL MAGIC I II III

By **Destiny Skai**

WHEN A GOOD GIRL GOES BAD

By **Adrienne**

THE COST OF LOYALTY I II III

By Kweli

A GANGSTER'S REVENGE **I II III & IV**

THE BOSS MAN'S DAUGHTERS I II III IV V

A SAVAGE LOVE **I & II**

BAE BELONGS TO ME I II

A HUSTLER'S DECEIT I, II, III

WHAT BAD BITCHES DO I, II, III

SOUL OF A MONSTER I II III

KILL ZONE

A DOPE BOY'S QUEEN I II III

TIL DEATH

By **Aryanna**

A KINGPIN'S AMBITON

A KINGPIN'S AMBITION **II**

I MURDER FOR THE DOUGH

By **Ambitious**

TRUE SAVAGE I II III IV V VI VII

DOPE BOY MAGIC I, II, III

MIDNIGHT CARTEL I II III

CITY OF KINGZ I II

NIGHTMARE ON SILENT AVE

THE PLUG OF LIL MEXICO I II

CLASSIC CITY

By **Chris Green**

A DOPEBOY'S PRAYER

The Black Diamond Cartel

By **Eddie "Wolf" Lee**

THE KING CARTEL **I, II & III**

By **Frank Gresham**

THESE NIGGAS AIN'T LOYAL **I, II & III**

By **Nikki Tee**

GANGSTA SHYT **I II &III**

By **CATO**

THE ULTIMATE BETRAYAL

By **Phoenix**

BOSS'N UP **I , II & III**

By **Royal Nicole**

I LOVE YOU TO DEATH

By **Destiny J**

I RIDE FOR MY HITTA

I STILL RIDE FOR MY HITTA

By **Misty Holt**

LOVE & CHASIN' PAPER

By **Qay Crockett**

TO DIE IN VAIN

SINS OF A HUSTLA

By **ASAD**

BROOKLYN HUSTLAZ

By **Boogsy Morina**

BROOKLYN ON LOCK I & II

By **Sonovia**

GANGSTA CITY

By **Teddy Duke**

A DRUG KING AND HIS DIAMOND I & II III

A DOPEMAN'S RICHES

HER MAN, MINE'S TOO I, II

SAYNOMORE

CASH MONEY HO'S
THE WIFEY I USED TO BE I II
PRETTY GIRLS DO NASTY THINGS
By Nicole Goosby
TRAPHOUSE KING **I II & III**
KINGPIN KILLAZ I II III
STREET KINGS I II
PAID IN BLOOD **I II**
CARTEL KILLAZ I II III
DOPE GODS I II
By **Hood Rich**
LIPSTICK KILLAH **I, II, III**
CRIME OF PASSION I II & III
FRIEND OR FOE I II III
By **Mimi**
STEADY MOBBN' **I, II, III**
THE STREETS STAINED MY SOUL I II III
By **Marcellus Allen**
WHO SHOT YA **I, II, III**
SON OF A DOPE FIEND I II
HEAVEN GOT A GHETTO I II
SKI MASK MONEY I II
Renta
GORILLAZ IN THE BAY **I II III IV**
TEARS OF A GANGSTA I II
3X KRAZY I II
STRAIGHT BEAST MODE I II
DE'KARI
TRIGGADALE I II III
MURDAROBER WAS THE CASE I II

The Black Diamond Cartel

Elijah R. Freeman
GOD BLESS THE TRAPPERS I, II, III
THESE SCANDALOUS STREETS I, II, III
FEAR MY GANGSTA I, II, III IV, V
THESE STREETS DON'T LOVE NOBODY I, II
BURY ME A G I, II, III, IV, V
A GANGSTA'S EMPIRE I, II, III, IV
THE DOPEMAN'S BODYGAURD I II
THE REALEST KILLAZ I II III
THE LAST OF THE OGS I II III
Tranay Adams
THE STREETS ARE CALLING
Duquie Wilson
MARRIED TO A BOSS I II III
By Destiny Skai & Chris Green
KINGZ OF THE GAME I II III IV V VI VII
CRIME BOSS
Playa Ray
SLAUGHTER GANG I II III
RUTHLESS HEART I II III
By Willie Slaughter
FUK SHYT
By Blakk Diamond
DON'T F#CK WITH MY HEART I II
By Linnea
ADDICTED TO THE DRAMA I II III
IN THE ARM OF HIS BOSS II
By Jamila
YAYO I II III IV
A SHOOTER'S AMBITION I II

SAYNOMORE

BRED IN THE GAME
By S. Allen
TRAP GOD I II III
RICH $AVAGE I II III
MONEY IN THE GRAVE I II III
By Martell Troublesome Bolden
FOREVER GANGSTA I II
GLOCKS ON SATIN SHEETS I II
By Adrian Dulan
TOE TAGZ I II III IV
LEVELS TO THIS SHYT I II
IT'S JUST ME AND YOU I II
By Ah'Million
KINGPIN DREAMS I II III
RAN OFF ON DA PLUG
By Paper Boi Rari
CONFESSIONS OF A GANGSTA I II III IV
CONFESSIONS OF A JACKBOY I II
By Nicholas Lock
I'M NOTHING WITHOUT HIS LOVE
SINS OF A THUG
TO THE THUG I LOVED BEFORE
A GANGSTA SAVED XMAS
IN A HUSTLER I TRUST
By Monet Dragun
CAUGHT UP IN THE LIFE I II III
THE STREETS NEVER LET GO I II III
By Robert Baptiste
NEW TO THE GAME I II III
MONEY, MURDER & MEMORIES I II III

The Black Diamond Cartel

By **Malik D. Rice**
LIFE OF A SAVAGE I II III IV
A GANGSTA'S QUR'AN I II III IV
MURDA SEASON I II III
GANGLAND CARTEL I II III
CHI'RAQ GANGSTAS I II III IV
KILLERS ON ELM STREET I II III
JACK BOYZ N DA BRONX I II III
A DOPEBOY'S DREAM I II III
JACK BOYS VS DOPE BOYS I II III
COKE GIRLZ
COKE BOYS
SOSA GANG I II III
BRONX SAVAGES
BODYMORE KINGPINS
BLOOD OF A GOON
By **Romell Tukes**
LOYALTY AIN'T PROMISED I II
By **Keith Williams**
QUIET MONEY I II III
THUG LIFE I II III
EXTENDED CLIP I II
A GANGSTA'S PARADISE
By **Trai'Quan**
THE STREETS MADE ME I II III
By **Larry D. Wright**
THE ULTIMATE SACRIFICE I, II, III, IV, V, VI
KHADIFI
IF YOU CROSS ME ONCE I II
ANGEL I II III IV

SAYNOMORE

IN THE BLINK OF AN EYE
By **Anthony Fields**
THE LIFE OF A HOOD STAR
By Ca$h & Rashia Wilson
THE STREETS WILL NEVER CLOSE I II III
By K'ajji
CREAM I II III
THE STREETS WILL TALK
By Yolanda Moore
NIGHTMARES OF A HUSTLA I II III
BLOOD AND GAMES
By King Dream
CONCRETE KILLA I II III
VICIOUS LOYALTY I II III
By Kingpen
HARD AND RUTHLESS I II
MOB TOWN 251
THE BILLIONAIRE BENTLEYS I II III
REAL G'S MOVE IN SILENCE
By Von Diesel
GHOST MOB
Stilloan Robinson
MOB TIES I II III IV V VI
SOUL OF A HUSTLER, HEART OF A KILLER I II III
GORILLAZ IN THE TRENCHES I II III
THE BLACK DIAMOND CARTEL
By SayNoMore
BODYMORE MURDERLAND I II III
THE BIRTH OF A GANGSTER I II
By Delmont Player

194

The Black Diamond Cartel

FOR THE LOVE OF A BOSS

By C. D. Blue

MOBBED UP I II III IV

THE BRICK MAN I II III IV V

THE COCAINE PRINCESS I II III IV V VI VII VIII IX

SUPER GREMLIN

By King Rio

KILLA KOUNTY I II III IV

By Khufu

MONEY GAME I II

By Smoove Dolla

A GANGSTA'S KARMA I II III

By FLAME

KING OF THE TRENCHES I II III

by **GHOST & TRANAY ADAMS**

QUEEN OF THE ZOO I II

By **Black Migo**

GRIMEY WAYS I II III

By Ray Vinci

XMAS WITH AN ATL SHOOTER

By Ca$h & Destiny Skai

KING KILLA

By Vincent "Vitto" Holloway

BETRAYAL OF A THUG I II

By Fre$h

THE MURDER QUEENS I II III

By Michael Gallon

TREAL LOVE

By Le'Monica Jackson

FOR THE LOVE OF BLOOD I II III

SAYNOMORE

By Jamel Mitchell
HOOD CONSIGLIERE I II
By Keese
PROTÉGÉ OF A LEGEND I II III
LOVE IN THE TRENCHES
By Corey Robinson
BORN IN THE GRAVE I II III
By Self Made Tay
MOAN IN MY MOUTH
SANCTIFIED AND HORNY
By XTASY
TORN BETWEEN A GANGSTER AND A GENTLEMAN
By J-BLUNT & Miss Kim
LOYALTY IS EVERYTHING I II
Molotti
HERE TODAY GONE TOMORROW
By Fly Rock
PILLOW PRINCESS
By S. Hawkins
NAÏVE TO THE STREETS
WOMEN LIE MEN LIE I II III
GIRLS FALL LIKE DOMINOS
STACK BEFORE YOU SPURLGE
FIFTY SHADES OF SNOW I II III
By A. Roy Milligan
SALUTE MY SAVAGERY
By Fumiya Payne

The Black Diamond Cartel

BOOKS BY LDP'S CEO, CA$H

TRUST IN NO MAN

TRUST IN NO MAN 2

TRUST IN NO MAN 3

BONDED BY BLOOD

SHORTY GOT A THUG

THUGS CRY

THUGS CRY 2

THUGS CRY 3

TRUST NO BITCH

TRUST NO BITCH 2

TRUST NO BITCH 3

TIL MY CASKET DROPS

RESTRAINING ORDER

RESTRAINING ORDER 2

IN LOVE WITH A CONVICT

LIFE OF A HOOD STAR

XMAS WITH AN ATL SHOOTER

SAYNOMORE